"Easily the craziest, weirdest, strangest, funniest, most obscene writer in America."
—*GOTHIC MAGAZINE*

"Carlton Mellick III has the craziest book titles... and the kinkiest fans!"
—CHRISTOPHER MOORE, author of *The Stupidest Angel*

"If you haven't read Mellick you're not nearly perverse enough for the twenty first century."
—JACK KETCHUM, author of *The Girl Next Door*

"Carlton Mellick III is one of bizarro fiction's most talented practitioners, a virtuoso of the surreal, science fictional tale."
—CORY DOCTOROW, author of *Little Brother*

"Bizarre, twisted, and emotionally raw—Carlton Mellick's fiction is the literary equivalent of putting your brain in a blender."
—BRIAN KEENE, author of *The Rising*

"Carlton Mellick III exemplifies the intelligence and wit that lurks between its lurid covers. In a genre where crude titles are an art in themselves, Mellick is a true artist."
—*THE GUARDIAN*

"Just as Pop had Andy Warhol and Dada Tristan Tzara, the bizarro movement has its very own P. T. Barnum-type practitioner. He's the mutton-chopped author of such books as *Electric Jesus Corpse* and *The Menstruating Mall*, the illustrator, editor, and instructor of all things bizarro, and his name is Carlton Mellick III."
—*DETAILS MAGAZINE*

Also by
Carlton Mellick III

Satan Burger
Electric Jesus Corpse (Fan Club Exclusive)
Sunset With a Beard (stories)
Razor Wire Pubic Hair
Teeth and Tongue Landscape
The Steel Breakfast Era
The Baby Jesus Butt Plug
Fishy-fleshed
The Menstruating Mall
Ocean of Lard (with Kevin L. Donihe)
Punk Land
Sex and Death in Television Town
Sea of the Patchwork Cats
The Haunted Vagina
Cancer-cute (Fan Club Exclusive)
War Slut
Sausagey Santa
Ugly Heaven
Adolf in Wonderland
Ultra Fuckers
Cybernetrix
The Egg Man
Apeshit
The Faggiest Vampire
The Cannibals of Candyland
Warrior Wolf Women of the Wasteland
The Kobold Wizard's Dildo of Enlightenment +2
Zombies and Shit

EVERY TIME WE MEET AT THE DAIRY QUEEN YOUR WHOLE FUCKING FACE EXPLODES

CARLTON MELLICK III

ERASERHEAD PRESS
PORTLAND, OREGON

ERASERHEAD PRESS
205 NE BRYANT
PORTLAND, OR 97211

WWW.ERASERHEADPRESS.COM

ISBN: 978-1-62105-221-0

AUTHOR'S NOTE

When I was in third grade, I had a crush on a girl named Dawn Sprinkle. She was kind of the weird girl in school. She had a squeaky high-pitched voice, was kind of short and skinny, had four leaf clover patches sewn into her jeans, and looked kind of like a Gelfling from the Jim Henson movie *The Dark Crystal*. If anyone in school was actually a fairy or an elf in human disguise it would have been her.

She used to sit next to me on the bus on the way to school every day. No matter how many seats were open on the bus, she would always sit right next to me. I felt like the most special boy in the school because of this. Of all the people to sit with, she chose me. We would inch closer to each other throughout the bus ride. But we never spoke to each other. We were two of the shyest kids in school. She was a rich kid who was obviously sheltered by strict parents, the kind who was too wrapped up in violin lessons and ballet recitals to have much of a social life outside of school. And I had a mother who lived in constant fear of her son being horribly murdered if I ever left the house for more than five minutes, so I spent most of my childhood locked away safely in my bedroom to write stories and make up imaginary friends. When I came up with the idea for this book, I was immediately reminded of what it was like to be a weird kid in love with the other weird kid in school. This story is pretty similar to my real life experiences, with a few exceptions. For instance, I was in third grade when this all happened, not junior high. And we never went on dates at the Dairy Queen. It's also important to point out that the girl I liked did not suffer from the same face-exploding condition as the girl in this book. She did, however, turn out to be an alien from outer space. And after all those months of sitting so close to her on the bus I accidentally contracted a weird space disease that caused me to grow thousands of tiny eyeballs all over my body.

It was pretty uncomfortable and painful to deal with eyeball skin. I still get outbreaks from time to time. And let me tell you, that shit is worse than herpes. I pretty much have to bathe in saline solution three times a day and getting pinkeye turns me into a giant ball of morning eye crust. Anyway, this story is kind of a cautionary tale for all those who fall in love for the first time. Be careful. That cute and quirky person you're crushing on might just turn out to be some kind of face-exploding eyeball-disease-infecting mutant alien who ends up fucking you up for the rest of your life. Of course, you don't really have a choice when it comes to who you fall in love with. Once it happens, there's no escape.

I hope you enjoy my new book. Written at a beach house retreat in 2015 with my author friends Vince Kramer, Gary Arthur Brown, and J. David Osborne, it has quickly become one of my personal favorites.

—Carlton Mellick III, 3/20/2016 3:29am

CHAPTER
ONE

She is the cutest girl in school. The one with the kitty-cat smile and four leaf clover barrettes. Two cherry-red pigtails flow down her back like electric eels dipped in Hawaiian Punch. Her bright green lipstick is sour-apple flavored and her favorite color of clothing is lime sherbet. And her eyes—two deep brown orbs that are so big you can see them from across the lunch room, staring at you when she thinks you don't notice.

Although she's the cutest, she's not liked by many of the boys in my class. Most of the kids I know think she's weird and annoying. Maybe because she's so twitchy and fidgety all the time. She can't sit still for even a second. It's like she's so caffeinated that it's as if she has a constant stream of fizzy pink energy drinks flowing into her system. She hops up and down in her seat when drawing in Art class, tick-tocks her head from side to side when flipping through the pages of Tom Sawyer during English. Sometimes her jittery movements are such a distraction that Mrs. Burcham makes her sit out in the hallway to work by herself.

But it's not just her twitchiness that makes everyone think she's weird. She's also rather clumsy and breaks everything she touches. She accidently blackened Big Mark Henney's eye by raising her hand too quickly during math time. She accidently dissected her middle finger while trying to dissect a frog in science class. The art room hamster was crushed to death when she stacked too many heavy books on the shelf above its cage. These things always happen when she's around. I think it's because she's always in her own world, daydreaming and unable to focus on anything around her.

One time, she was so stuck inside her head that she didn't notice a black widow spider that dropped on her shoulder during P.E. class. It was crawling all over her body for the rest of day, climbing up her back, hiding in her pigtails, dangling from her elbows by a long sticky thread. Everyone else could see it on her, but nobody bothered to tell her it was there. She didn't even notice on the bus ride home, sitting there with the spider perched happily on top of her head like a pet canary.

Ever since then, there's been a rumor going around that she's in love with spiders and wears them like accessories. At any given time, spiders might be crawling on her skin or hiding in her clothes. It is believed that if any boy ever tries to hug or kiss her they will surely be bit by one of the many poisonous spiders that call her home. This is how she gained the nickname *Spiderweb*—because spiders live on her like a human web.

Although the other boys stay far away from Spiderweb, I've been in love with her since the first day I saw her. On the bus ride to school one day, I watched as she climbed up the steps with the biggest smile on her face. It was her first day of school, she had transferred from some rich girls' academy upstate. I usually didn't like sitting next to anyone on the bus. I always kept my backpack on the seat next to me, blocking anyone who might want to sit there. But when I saw her coming down the aisle, I moved my backpack and made eye contact with her. She sat down in the seat and kept glancing at me the whole way to school with her giant wild eyes. Although she opened her mouth several times as though she wanted to say something to me, she never spoke a word. And I was just as shy as she was. I just stared at my knuckles and inched closer to her on the seat, too nervous to introduce myself.

Every day from then on it went the same way. I'd save her a seat and we'd sit together all the way to school. But we never said a word to each other. We just sat there with our thighs pressed together, trying to come up with something to say. We'd catch glimpses of each other during class or at lunchtime, touch fingers whenever one of us was chosen to pass out papers to the rest of the class, and watch each other play basketball or volleyball from the outskirts of the court.

When I admitted to my friends that I had a crush on her, they all thought I was insane. They told me that Spiderweb would stick to me if I touched her and all of her spiders would crawl on my skin. But this wasn't enough to dissuade me. I didn't care what anyone thought. Spiderweb was the only girl I liked in the whole entire school.

11

One day, she asked me to be her boyfriend. Not in words. She passed me a note on the bus which explained how she felt and asked me if we could be a couple. I agreed with a nod and smile. Then we held hands the rest of the way home. We never spoke a word. We still have yet to say anything to each other, only communicating through notes or body language. But now we are officially boyfriend and girlfriend.

Being Spiderweb's boyfriend is the best. It's made me happier than I've ever been in my life. But there's a big problem. Every time we go on a date, her face explodes. I don't know how it happens. I don't understand what can possibly cause such a thing to occur. She just seems to get so excited that pressure builds behind her skin. Her cheeks boil, her forehead bubbles, steam sifts through her lips and nostrils. Then her whole fucking face explodes.

The first time it happened, I freaked. We met for a date at the Dairy Queen to have strawberry sundaes. Her smile was so wide that it made stretch marks in her skin. Her eyes so open they bulged out of her eye sockets. She was so cute and cartoonish. Even the pigtails caught in the back of her armpits, making her look like she had cherry-red armpit hair, were absolutely adorable.

She looked like she had something really important to say to me, something she'd been trying to say to me for days. But she couldn't stop smiling like a crazy person.

Her teeth were clenched so tightly together they made grinding noises, her green lipstick smudged on her chin. Feeling awkward just staring at her, I opened my mouth to speak. But before I could tell her how pretty I thought she looked, her face exploded.

Blood and chunks of flesh splattered against me, getting in my mouth and all over my clothes. Her lips stuck in my hair like two wads of chewing gum. Her nose dropped into her lap. One of her eyeballs landed in my strawberry sundae.

When I rubbed the gore from my eyes, I saw only a red mess left on her skull. One eyeball looking back at me in shock. She didn't say anything. She just grabbed her pieces of face and ran away, crying.

I wasn't the only one in the Dairy Queen who saw what happened. Many patrons stared at me as I sat there covered in the girl's blood, wondering what the heck was going on.

"I didn't do it," I announced to the ice cream shop. Then I fled.

The next day, things were different. Spiderweb sat down next to me on the bus as usual, but she seemed to ignore me. She wouldn't look me in the eyes. Her face was covered by her cherry-red hair, tilting down toward her twitching, nervous fingers in her lap. I was so worried about what had happened that I wanted to ask her how she was, but I couldn't get the words out. When I peeked through her strands of hair, I saw that her face had been put back together with stitches and staples. Skin had been grafted onto her face from a donor with a much darker complexion.

It wasn't that she was in pain or disgusted by her new sewn-together face. She was just embarrassed and ashamed of herself for exploding in front of me. I felt so bad that I knew I had to do something to make her feel better. When I took her hand and gave it a squeeze, her demeanor changed completely. She looked back at me with the brightest expression. Tears in her eyes, her smile pulling at the stitches that held her face together. And when she kissed me on the cheek, her stitches were itchy against my skin.

I wasn't sure how I felt about Spiderweb for a while after that. Before, I thought she was absolute perfection, even with all of her quirks. But once her face exploded and was sewn back together, I started to wonder if there really was something horribly wrong with her. I wondered if the other kids were right about her. I wondered if she was a freak.

But I didn't break up with her. There was still something about her that made me want to be her boyfriend. Even though her face was stitched together, she was still much cuter than the other girls in my class. I just needed to get to know her better, understand why she exploded and what I could do to prevent it from happening again.

We went on three more dates and her face exploded every single time. It became less shocking each time it happened. By the fourth date, even the employees at the Dairy Queen saw it coming and reacted as though it was perfectly commonplace. But every single time, Spiderweb was so embarrassed that she ran away. Her face falling off to expose her skinless skull was the same to her as ripping a hole in her pants to expose a pink pair of panties.

Every time it happened, she came back to school the next day with new skin stitched to her face. The other kids teased her even more after that. In addition to Spiderweb, they called her *Frankenstein* or *Patchwork Girl*. Sometimes they combined her nicknames into *Frankenspider* or *Patchwork Webs*. But the other kids never teased her directly, only behind her back. They were all terrified of her. And when I told my friends about how her face explodes whenever she gets too excited, she became even more terrifying to the student body.

It was much worse for me than it was for her. My friends stopped hanging around me. People started calling me *Spider Lover* or *Frankenstein's Bride*. Although they were too scared to harass *Spiderweb* to her face, they weren't afraid to push me up against the lockers after school ended. Big Mark Henney punched me in the stomach whenever the teachers weren't looking. The other kids threw spit-wads at me and stuffed rubber spiders down my pants. They all thought there must be something seriously wrong with me for liking the weird girl.

If all I did was hang out with Spiderweb at school I would've been happy to have been ostracized by the other kids. I didn't need other friends if she was my only friend.

But I was too scared to go near her at school. Not just because I was shy around her, I was also scared that she might explode again. I couldn't handle the embarrassment of causing her to explode during school hours.

We still sit together on the bus. We still pass notes to each other and watch each other from across the lunchroom. But that's the extent of our relationship. I can tell it makes her feel bad, ashamed of her sewn-together face and her spontaneous explosion problem. And I feel like such a jerk for not being brave enough to get too close.

But today is going to be different. Today I plan to spend time with her, treat her like a real boyfriend would treat her. I just have to figure out a way to be with her without making her face explode.

CHAPTER
TWO

When she comes onto the bus, I don't hide my head or stare at my hands as I usually do. I look her right in the eyes and smile as she comes toward me. She's greener than ever today, wearing her favorite St. Patrick's Day dress and glittery emerald-green shoes. Her makeup is the color of mint leaves. Even her eyebrows are colored a deep shade of green. She smiles back at me with her stitched-up face and sits down.

"Spider Lover!" somebody cries two seats back.

"They're *so* creepy..." a chubby girl whispers to her friends across the aisle.

But I ignore them. I take Spiderweb's hand in mine. This time I don't look away out of bashfulness. I maintain eye contact. This close, I can see all the details in her stitched-together face. Each piece of skin is a different color, all from different donors. She really looks like a patchwork quilt. But she's been put together so carefully that she doesn't look as grotesque as you'd think. The new pieces of skin don't overlap or bulge out in awkward places. When she heals, she won't have much scar tissue.

She'll still look patchy, but her skin will be smooth. Whatever doctor put her back together must be some kind of master surgeon.

I open my mouth to speak and hesitate for a second. But I won't wimp out. Not this time.

"Will you sit with me at lunch today?" I ask her.

Her face lights up and her mouth opens wide as if to say *yes*. But when the words don't come out, she nods her head four times. Then she squeezes my hand tightly.

That is the extent of our conversation, but it's enough to satisfy her for now. I'll talk to her more at lunchtime. I don't want her to ever have to spend another day alone at school.

She places her head on my shoulder, snuggles in with a creepy smile on her face. I'm not sure if it's just my imagination or not, but I swear I feel a spider crawling across the back of my neck.

During homeroom, Josh asks me, "Are you really going to sit next to *Spiderweb* at lunchtime?"

Josh was my best friend two weeks ago. Now he's my biggest bully and harasses me even more than Big Mark Henney. He sits behind me and shoves against the back of my chair to get my attention. He hates the fact that I like the weird girl more than I like him.

"Yeah, so what?" I say.

"She's going to eat your soul. She's going to put

spiders all over you and then drink your blood. Only an idiot would like a girl like her."

I slink down in my chair. Then say, "At least I have a girlfriend…"

"No, seriously. She looks like the Corpse Bride. Why are you in love with Corpse Bride?"

I don't respond. Just trying to do my homework while he kicks on the back of my seat.

"Are you going to marry her? Do you want her to be *your* Corpse Bride?"

"No…"

"Yeah, right. You probably fantasize about it every night with your hand under the covers."

"Shut up." I move to an empty desk in the back of the room, even though it's not my assigned seat. The teacher notices but doesn't say anything.

I don't care what Josh says to me. He's not going to get me to change how I feel about Spiderweb. I know he only bullies me so that the other kids won't bully him for being Spiderweb's boyfriend's best friend. He probably thinks that if he can break us up we'll be able to be friends again. But that's not going to happen. After all he's done, I don't want to be friends with him again even if I wasn't with Spiderweb.

I spend the next four periods preparing myself to talk to Spiderweb. I think about what I want to say to her, trying to find the perfect words. But the closer it gets to lunch, the more panicked I become. I really don't know what to say.

At lunchtime, I go straight to the bathroom and hide in one of the stalls, my heart racing in my chest. Part of me wants to just stay in the bathroom the whole lunch period and then make up an excuse about why I couldn't meet her. Maybe I suddenly got the flu and had to be sent home. Maybe one of the teachers forced me to stay behind after class. But then I think about how sad she would be if I didn't show. I made a promise to her. Even if I don't say anything, I should still sit next to her like I said I would.

"It doesn't matter what you talk about," I say to myself. "Just talk about anything."

Somebody bursts into laughter over by the urinals. I'm not alone in the bathroom.

I pause for a moment and listen carefully, wondering if I just imagined the laugh. The television once said that high anxiety can cause hallucinations like this, you can hear voices that aren't really there. The laugh could've been in my head.

Then the sound of a loud fart and urine hitting toilet water.

"Talking to yourself in there, Spider Lover," says the kid at the urinal.

I recognize the voice. Only one kid in school has a voice that deep. It's Mark Henney, the biggest kid in class. Being fifteen years old and still in the eighth grade has made him the one person you never want to piss off.

"Shit…" I whisper.

Of all people, it had to be him. The last time I found myself alone in a bathroom with Mark Henney, he tried to shove my face in a toilet that was filled with diarrhea. Some kid with stomach flu left it in there, too sick to even flush the toilet. Mark thought it was funny and wanted to put somebody's face in it. I happened to be in the wrong place at the wrong time.

The second I saw him looking at me from the toilet stall, laughing his ass off, I knew I was going to be his target. I rushed to the bathroom door, but before I could escape he grabbed me by my arm and dragged me across the floor, then kicked me in the stomach when I refused to get up. Mrs. Burcham heard me screaming and broke it up before anything happened. But I still left with a ripped shirt and bruises forming on my ribcage.

If he decides to mess with me now it could ruin things with Spiderweb. If he wedgies me or puts my face in the toilet, I'll be too embarrassed to let her see me.

"What are you doing, jerking off in there?" Mark asks.

I've got to get out of here before he finishes peeing. It's my only chance.

"I guess you'd have to be a pervert to be in love with Frankenstein."

I completely ignore Mark, don't even look at him as I leave the stall and go for the bathroom door.

"Where do you think you're going?"

Mark stops peeing midstream and steps away from the porcelain, blocking me from the bathroom door.

"Get out of my way," I tell him.

21

Mark smiles with crusty lips. Three large unpopped zits on his forehead glisten in the iridescent light.

"Not until you lick them," he says.

I shake my head, but don't make eye contact. "I'm late for lunch."

As I try to get around him, he leans all of his weight against the door. My only way out is through his brick wall of a body.

"I said not until you *lick* them," he says.

"Lick what?"

He laughs and drops his backpack, then pulls up his shirt to reveal three large growths poking out of his lower abdomen.

"What the fuck?" I cry, stepping away from him.

The growths are bright red and shaped like a cross between a rooster's wattle and deformed baby hands. I've heard of these before. Rumors about the disgusting tumors hiding under Mark Henney's shirt have been spreading all year, but I didn't know they were so big. They say his parents don't have health insurance and can't afford to get them removed. They also say that he's so insecure about them that he won't take his shirt off when he swims in a pool. Some even think he bullies kids just so they won't make fun of him. In junior high, it's better to be feared than laughed at.

"Why not?" he asks. "They're not any uglier than Frankenstein and you *love* to lick her."

He takes a step forward. I take a step back. He points the largest one in my direction.

"Get those things away from me," I say.

He laughs. "Why should I?"

"You're disgusting."

"Well, you're a pervert. Deep down, you probably *want* to lick them." He rubs the large growth. It becomes erect in his fingers, swelling larger with each stroke. "Come on. Give it a taste."

He laughs as I cringe at the sight of them. I realize the only way out of this is to talk him out of it.

"Come on, Mark. It's pizza day. If we don't hurry they're going to run out."

"I don't care."

"Yeah, you do. You like pizza more than anyone."

"Maybe I like getting my wobblies licked even more."

What did he just call them?

"Wobblies?" I ask.

"Yeah." He shakes his large growth. "Wobblies."

As he steps toward me, away from the door, I try to make a break for it. I run around him, but he pins me against the wall. His wobblies touching my arm.

"Come on," he says, pushing me into the tiled wall with all of his weight. "Lick them and get it over with. If I miss pizza day I'm going to kick your ass."

As I struggle to get out of his grip, I feel the growth swelling against my arm. It's oddly warm, like a water balloon filled with hot jelly.

"Get off me," I cry.

He shoves my face toward the tumor. "Not until you lick one."

As he rubs himself against my forearm, a thick mucus-like substance squirts out the tip of his tumor onto my arm. He moans at the sensation, pressing himself harder against me. A smell similar to Taco Bell meat fills the bathroom as the mucus oozes down his waist.

I cry, "You're such a…"

But before I finish, the bathroom door opens and hits me in the shoulder, knocking me away from Mark.

"Whoa!" a voice echoes into the bathroom. "Out of my way!"

It's Tony, the fat Apache kid. He shoves his way into the bathroom, carrying a rectangular piece of pizza in a napkin. His bulging belly hangs from a bright yellow Kool & the Gang T-shirt.

Mark turns his back and tucks his shirt into his pants, embarrassed about Tony seeing his tumors.

"What's up, fat ass?" Mark asks.

"Gotta take a dump," Tony says, laughing. Then he takes a bite of his pizza and heads toward the nearest bathroom stall.

Tony is the second biggest kid in school and the only one who's not afraid of Mark. Even though he's almost a foot shorter, Tony probably weighs a lot more. They're not friends or enemies, but people have been betting on which of them would win in a fight if they were ever to piss each other off. My money would be on Tony. Not because he's stronger, but because he's not insecure about anything. He doesn't need to pick on smaller kids to prove he's a badass.

I use the opportunity to sneak out of the room while Mark's distracted, wiping the tumor fluid against my thigh.

When I look back into the bathroom from the hallway, Mark stares me down. With a wet spot spreading across the lower part of his shirt, Mark says, "I'll get you later, Spider Lover."

Then I take off for the cafeteria.

CHAPTER
THREE

Spiderweb smiles at me from across the lunchroom and all thoughts of Big Mark Henney disappear from my head. She sits by herself at a table far away from the other students, saving my seat with her Fern Gully backpack in the same way I've always saved her seat on the bus. There's no point for her to be saving my seat, though. No other kid in school would ever want to sit anywhere near her. But the gesture made my heart flutter like a moth on a light bulb.

I wave at her, trying to ignore the table full of girls laughing at the wet spot on my thigh. Then I go to get some pizza before it runs out. The lunch line is pretty short now, so it only takes me a few minutes to get through. The only piece left by the time I get to the counter is a deformed triangular end piece that was folded up against the edge of the tray.

"That's all we got," the lunch lady says, rubbing a hairy mole on her chin, totally unapologetic that she just charged me five bucks for a miserable chunk of pizza mush.

I take my tray to Spiderweb's table, but she forgets to remove her backpack from the seat she saved for me. She just smiles up at me when I arrive. Her stitched-up face gleams, reflecting the light off of shiny oils on her face. With her backpack blocking the spot at the table next to her, I sit one chair away.

We don't make eye contact, just taking bites of pizza, glancing over her backpack at each other between bites, waiting for the other to speak. But neither of us know what to say.

She eats around the outside of her pizza until it forms the shape of a heart. Then she smiles at me. It's how she always eats her food. I've seen her do it before. With sandwiches, hamburgers, lasagna, and even tacos. She takes bites until her food is the shape of a heart. Then she throws it away, leaving the heart-shaped food on the top of the trash pile so everyone can see it on their way outside.

"What the f—" Mark Henney yells across the lunch room.

I look up to see him at the lunchroom counter, realizing they're out of pizza. He immediately locks eyes with mine and just shakes his head at me. As though saying, "You are so dead."

It's his own fault for harassing me in the bathroom. If he left me alone we both would have gotten fresh hot rectangles of pizza. Now he's stuck eating a soy butter and jelly sandwich.

He looks like he's about to come over to me and

take the pizza off of my plate. But halfway across the cafeteria, he sees who's sitting next to me. Even Big Mark Henney won't go anywhere near Spiderweb. He breaks eye contact and goes after another kid's pizza, whispering something threatening into his ear until he hands his lunch over to him.

With Mark Henney scared of her, being next to Spiderweb is the safest place I could be. I wonder if I should hang out with her as much as possible. Then maybe people would leave me alone.

I inch closer to her, trying to think of something to say.

"I like your backpack," I tell her.

Her multi-colored cheeks blush.

In the quietest voice, she says, "Thanks."

Then she realizes her backpack is preventing us from sitting closer together and moves it to the other side of her food tray. I get up and switch seats, sitting closer to her. But once I see the skin of her face beginning to boil, I scoot my chair a few inches back. The last thing I want is to make her face explode in the middle of the cafeteria.

The other kids stare at us, giggling and pointing. Because we're surrounded by empty chairs and tables, it feels like we're on a stage, surrounded by a large audience. Everyone knows we're a couple, but nobody's ever seen us with each other except for the kids who ride our bus. Because they've not seen us together, some of them probably doubted the rumors were true. But now they've got proof with their own eyes. By sitting next to Spiderweb, I'm making a statement: she's my girlfriend and I don't care who knows about it. It's about time I did this. I don't want Spiderweb to think

I've never sat next to her because I was embarrassed to admit I'm her boyfriend.

"I like your hair," I tell her.

It's the same hair she always has, but I don't know what else to say to her.

She smiles and says, "Thank you," pulling on one of her Cherry Kool-Aid pigtails. "I do them myself."

There's something wrong with Spiderweb's voice. Although she hasn't spoken to me much before, I've heard her speak during class many times, so I'm very familiar with how she usually speaks. But now her voice is different. It sounds kind of alien, like ET. The last time her face exploded, it also took out part of her neck. I wonder if her larynx was damaged. Perhaps her voice box had to be replaced with someone else's.

I nod at her. "I like red hair."

She nods back.

My messy piece of pizza is hardly edible. It looks like it was turned inside-out. Sauce gets all over my mouth and fingers whenever I try to take a bite. My napkin quickly becomes a useless crumpled up ball. I decide not to eat anymore so that Spiderweb doesn't think I'm messy and gross.

She doesn't look like she's going to eat anymore either, her pizza now perfectly heart-shaped. We just stare at our food for a while, barely speaking to each other.

Then I ask, "Can we sit together at lunch again tomorrow?"

She shakes her head no.

It surprises me. My voice becomes shaky. I don't

29

understand why she wouldn't want to sit next to me again. Is it embarrassing having everyone looking at us and laughing? Does she not really like me like I thought she did?

"Not just tomorrow." She smiles at me, then places her heart-shaped pizza on my plate. "Every day."

After lunch, I don't want to go hang out on the basketball court with all the other kids. I ask Spiderweb if she wants to hang out with me in the music room. She thinks it's a great idea.

Mrs. Jennings leaves the music room open at lunch so the band kids can practice, but they never want to waste their lunch hour on school stuff so the room is always empty. Spiderweb and I can hang out together without being made fun of.

We hold hands on the way to the music room, ignoring the snickering students we pass in the hallway. But once we get in the room and are completely alone, we don't really know what to do there. We still don't quite know what to say to each other.

"What's your favorite band?" I ask her.

She shrugs. "I don't know. Pop Atari."

I nod. I have no idea what that band is.

"What's your favorite television show?" she asks.

"Animal Man," I say.

She nods and looks away. She obviously has no clue

30

what show I'm talking about.

After a few moments of awkward silence, she says, "You can kiss me if you want to."

Did I just hear that correctly? Did she just want me to kiss her?

"Uhhh…"

She blushes and looks away. "You don't have to if you don't want to…"

"No," I say.

The instant I say *no*, her expression droops, like she's about to cry. She thinks I'm rejecting her.

I step closer and say, "I mean, of course I want to… But is it okay?"

Just going on a date made her face explode. I can't imagine what would happen if I try to kiss her.

She shrugs. "I don't know."

"But you want to try anyway?" I ask.

She looks me in the eyes and nods.

Then she says, "Maybe… it doesn't matter?"

"What do you mean it doesn't matter? Doesn't it hurt when you…"

I don't want to use the word *explode*. I know she's sensitive about it.

"Yeah, it hurts a little," she says. "But maybe… it'll be worth it?"

A creepy smile curls across her lips. I don't know what to think about her response. She's okay with having her face explode? She'd rather kiss me and have it happen than not kiss me at all? It's kind of insane that she feels this way. Even though I'm in love with Spiderweb, I don't know if I'd be willing to kiss her if the same thing happened to my face.

I shake my head. "I don't want to hurt you."

Her sad face returns.

"Forget it," she says.

She hides her face in her hair, trying to hold back tears. Then she goes for the door. It's obvious that she's embarrassed I turned her down. Even though my reason for not kissing her is because I'm worried about her face exploding, she's reacting as though it's more than that. Like I think her stitched-up face isn't attractive enough for me to kiss. Or that I'll think she's gross if her face explodes. But I can't let her think I really feel this way.

Before she leaves the room, I say, "Wait."

She stops and slowly turns around.

"We can try…" I say.

The smile returns to her face.

I continue, "But if it seems like it's about to happen again, we have to stop."

She nods her head in agreement. "Okay."

Then she closes eyes and purses her lips at me, waiting for me to kiss her.

I've only kissed a girl once before, in the 3rd grade. But that didn't really count. I only did it on a dare. It was Tiff Shipley, the tomboy in school, who used to get into fights with boys that she liked. When a rumor went around that she had a crush on me, my friends persuaded me to kiss her. They wanted to see her beat me up. But it didn't turn out the way they thought it would. I kissed her as she went down the slide, then I ran away. She chased me all over the playground. But when she caught me she didn't beat me up. She just kissed me back and said we were even. It turned out she didn't like me after all.

Kissing Tiff Shipley was scary, but not nearly as much as kissing Spiderweb. Partially because I actually love Spiderweb and have been waiting all year to kiss her and don't want to mess it up. But also because her face will very likely explode. It is like kissing a ticking time bomb.

I take slow steps toward her, watching every detail of her face. With her eyes closed, I think I might have a chance. Perhaps if I kiss her quickly, before she knows it, her face won't explode on me. But once I'm within two feet, she senses my presence. Her pursed lips curl into a smile. Her eyelids flutter over her large bulging eyes. Then her skin begins to boil.

"Wait." I step back and hold off until the boiling calms down.

She doesn't open her eyes, still waiting for me. "It's okay."

I step even slower this time, trying to be as quiet as possible. Like a snake creeping up on a jittery squirrel. I get within a foot of her lips before her face boils again. I move back.

"Just do it," she says.

I realize going slow might be the wrong way to do this. I'm creating too much anticipation, causing her thoughts and emotions to race through her head. This is likely why her face bubbles up on me. If I just rush in and kiss her and then pull away, it will all be fine.

"Okay…" I say, taking a deep breath.

Then I rush at her and kiss her on the lips.

Once her skin starts to bubble against my cheeks, I try to push away, but she doesn't let me go. She wraps her arms around me, gripping the back of my neck and holding me tightly against her. She kisses me back, pressing her itchy stitches into my mouth. I don't know what to do. I hug her around the waist and let her probe my mouth with her long pointy tongue. But with every second we kiss, the bubbles move faster beneath her skin. It feels like thousands of maggots are crawling inside of her.

I try to pull away, try to tell her to stop, but every time I open my mouth she just shoves her tongue down my throat making it impossible to get words out. There's nothing I can do to prevent it. Her skin swells and vibrates like a miniature volcano ready to erupt.

When her face explodes, it's like a cherry bomb going off in my mouth. Hundreds of flesh-bullets tear through me, ripping open my cheeks and lips. My nose cracks. I nearly choke on her tongue as it launches toward the back of my throat. The force of the explosion knocks me off my feet and throws me into the stack of drums and cymbals on the other side of the room. Spiderweb is tossed over a row of chairs and takes three of them with her on the way to the floor.

When we come to, both of us are covered in blood. Chunks of wet sticky flesh coats our bodies. The explosion was bigger than all of the others combined. It was like a grenade went off in the room. Both of us are severely injured from it.

But when I look over at Spiderweb, she just smiles and giggles as though nothing serious happened. She doesn't run away in embarrassment this time. She's happy. Her bloody skull glows with delight at just having kissed a boy for the first time. The sight of her skeletal face giggling at me sends shivers down my spine.

CHAPTER
FOUR

We sit in the nurse's office together, holding hands, waiting for Spiderweb's dad to pick her up and take her to the emergency room. The school nurse is too frightened to even look at us. We went to the nurse's office with our faces covered by our jackets and backpacks so nobody would see us or make fun of us. But once the cheerful nurse saw our injuries, she nearly fainted. She had a panic attack and ran out of the office, ready to call the police. But I calmed her and told her this was normal. She hasn't come within ten feet of us ever since.

"Here," I say to Spiderweb, handing her the severed tongue I pulled out of my mouth. "This came off in me."

She takes the tongue and puts it in her coat pocket and then squeezes my hand twice. Without her tongue, she's not able to speak.

I try not to look directly at her face. It's more messed up than ever before. So much flesh is missing from her head that I can see the bone of her skull through the gore. One of her eyeballs popped in its socket. There's no way that's going to be repaired. I guess I'm now going to be the boyfriend of a one-eyed girl. But I guess being called *pirate lover* isn't any worse than *spider lover* or *Frankenstein's Bride.*

We just sit here. Waiting. Holding hands. Blood dripping down our faces. Our hearts fluttering in our chests. It wasn't what I was expecting our first kiss to be like. Back when I first met her, before I knew about her exploding face problem, I imagined our first kiss would be magical and heavenly. I even imagined it to be explosive, just not *literally* explosive. It was morbid and painful. But, for some reason, I don't regret it. Everything up until the explosion was even more enjoyable than I expected, even with the stitches in her lips. I think I truly love Spiderweb. Even with her skin missing from her face, I still can't let go of her hand.

A tall man with thick glasses and a clean suit enters the nurse's office. It's Spiderweb's father—a very serious, intimidating figure. He looks down at her, then glares at me, then goes back to his daughter.

"Look at this…" he says in a deep, severe tone.

He looks like he's about to strangle me. Like it was all my fault his daughter exploded and he's going to do horrible things to get back at me. He eyeballs my condition, casting a shadow over my whole body, leaning down to investigate the damaged sections of my face.

Then he looks at his daughter and his demeanor

changes. A big smile appears on his face.

"My little girl's in love!" he cries.

Then he hugs her and kisses her skinless cheek. My mouth drops open. I can't believe he's reacting this way. It's like he's happy this happened.

"Your first kiss," he tells her. "Your mother's going to be so proud of you. You're all grown up!"

I quickly realize there's something seriously wrong with her family. No normal parent would react with joy at seeing their child's face completely blown off.

He turns to me. "You must be Ethan."

When he holds out his hand to shake, I hesitate for a moment. When I take his hand, it's cold and dry, both firm and smooth like his palm is made entirely of scar tissue.

"Uh… yeah," I say, as he shakes my hand up and down.

"I'm Stephen. *So* nice to meet you." He smiles again. His smile is even bigger than his daughter's. "Our little Spiderweb has told us all about you."

Wait, did he just call her Spiderweb? Her real name is Jill. Spiderweb's just a cruel nickname. Why would he call her that?

"You don't know how excited we all are that you two are in love with each other," Stephen says. "A girl like Spidie is incomplete without a boy in her life. She was only half a person until she chose you to be her other half."

The conversation is quickly getting awkward. I've never heard of a father so invested in his thirteen-year-old daughter's love life. And why would she be incomplete without a boyfriend? Does he think of girls as helpless sub-humans who can't handle the world without a man by their side? This man worries me even more than his daughter's exploding face.

He turns to Spiderweb, "Well, let's go home and get you stitched up." He looks at me and examines my face. "It looks like you could use some repairs yourself. You should come, too."

The thought of going home with this man makes my knees shake. "Shouldn't we go to the emergency room?"

He shakes his head. "No need. Our house is fully equipped for reconstructive surgery. Besides, hospitals are expensive. And I'm sure Sarah would love to meet you."

"Sarah?" I ask.

"Jill's mother," he says. "She's probably more excited about you falling in love with our daughter than anyone. She's always wanted a son."

After he says that, I realize it's best if I don't go home with them. I love Spiderweb. I don't care about her exploding face or quirky personality. I don't think she's a freak. But her family is a different story. Just five minutes with her father and I already think they have to be a family of psychopaths.

"I think I should call my parents," I say. "They'll want me to go to the hospital."

I stand up, wanting to leave the room to go for the receptionist's desk. But the father blocks my path.

"Nonsense," he says. "I'll fix you up and then you'll stay for dinner. I won't take no for an answer."

"But—" I begin.

Stephen cuts me off. "Come. You can sit in the back seat together so you can hold hands the whole way home."

I back away. "Umm…"

I try to figure a way out of it, scanning my brain for some kind of excuse. But once Spiderweb stands up and grabs me by the hand, laying her gory face against my shoulder, I realize there's no way out. I've got to go home with them.

The whole ride to their house, Spiderweb presses her bloody face against mine, poking her cheekbone into me. Because her face already exploded, she's able to get as close to me as she wants without worrying it will happen again. She uses the opportunity to wrap her arms around me, weaving her legs through mine, holding me so tightly like she never plans to let me go. This would have been heaven to me if her face wasn't in its current state. I feel like I'm being groped by a flesh-eating zombie.

The father doesn't do anything to stop us from showing such up-close affection in the backseat. He just blares an old Van Halen tape, singing along to the lyrics. Between songs, he looks back at us in the rearview mirror and says, "Oh, so cute," or "my precious little girl," and then continues singing.

When we get to their house, the place is even bigger than I expected it would be. I knew Spiderweb lived on the upper class side of town, but I had no idea she lived in a house this size. Fourteen of my houses could easily fit inside of hers, and my house is the biggest one on my block. I had no idea what Stephen did for a living, but they were obviously one of the wealthiest families in town. The driveway alone takes four minutes to travel down. We park in one of the three garages on the property.

"Let's go, kids," Stephen says, leading us out of the car into the house.

The front room is the size of a hotel lobby, full of decorative couches and tables. Original paintings by famous artists hang on the walls. Crystal chandeliers dangle from the four-story-high ceiling. Everything is brand new. The place seems recently built, like Spiderweb's family are the first people who ever lived here. They likely designed the house themselves.

There's something wrong with the house. I can't put my finger on it. It's clean, but too clean. Nice, but too nice. It doesn't seem like the kind of place anyone lives in. More like a model of a home, inhabited only by porcelain dolls and plastic golden retrievers.

"Sarah's upstairs," Stephen says. "She's going to be so surprised."

He takes off his coat and hat, hangs them in a closet larger than my bedroom. Then he goes to the edge of the staircase and yells up, "Sarah, are you up there? We have a visitor."

He turns to me and says, "Stand here." He takes my hand and pulls me into the center of the room. Then he puts Spiderweb beside me and forces our hands together, positioning us like we're posing for a photograph. "Just like this."

Then he goes back to the staircase and calls up to her again.

I look over at Spiderweb's skull poking out of her gory face. The blood is drying on her bones. I can't help but wonder why he isn't getting help for her. It's like her faceless skull is a completely normal sight to them. Spiderweb just stands there, jittering with excitement.

A dark form appears at the top of the stairs, moving slowly, using a cane to take careful steps. I'm guessing it is Spiderweb's mother, but from this angle I can't make out any features. She's more like a ghost or a walking corpse. She doesn't come down. I'm not sure her fragile form is capable of making it down the steps on her own.

Stephen smiles and points at me. "Sarah, this is Ethan. You've heard about Ethan, haven't you? Our little girl has a boyfriend of her very own."

When the woman steps into the light, I see her more clearly. She looks nothing like Spiderweb. In fact, she barely looks human. She wears only a robe that hangs slightly open, exposing her patchwork flesh. Her whole body is like Spiderweb's face—a collection of stitched-together skin from various donors. She must have the same exploding disease as Spiderweb, only she's been exploding and getting stitched together for decades. She doesn't have any hair on her head, like her face has exploded so many times she can no longer grow hair of her own. And even her explosions weren't restricted to just her face. Her whole body has burst apart several times.

I wonder if Spiderweb will someday become like this creature looking down at me. If she gets excited enough, will her whole body explode and need to be stitched together? Or is Spiderweb's exploding disease not as bad as her mother's?

"A pleasure, young man," the woman says. Her voice a raspy croak through her damaged voice box.

She doesn't come down to greet me. She just stares at me, examining my body, not speaking another word.

"Hi," I say to her. It's all I can think of to say.

She nods and returns to her room.

Stephen squeezes my shoulder and says, "You've made her so happy. I haven't seen her this excited in ages."

But I don't know what he's talking about. She didn't look happy or excited to me. She looked lethargic and disinterested. Perhaps she doesn't wear her emotions in the same way Stephen and Spiderweb do.

"Let's get you both fixed up," he says. "Then I'll prepare dinner. We're having meat rolls. Do you like meat rolls?"

I shrug. I have no idea what meat rolls are. Spiderweb bounces up and down when her father mentions dinner, her gory skull face gleaming with excitement. Meat rolls must be one of her favorites.

"You'll love it," Stephen says.

Then he takes Spiderweb away, deep into their compound-sized home, to reconstruct her face.

CHAPTER
FIVE

I am left in some kind of entertainment room. It's not a living room or family room. It's more of a waiting room for house guests, filled with board games, books, puzzles, and a television set. Stephen didn't say how long he was going to be with Spiderweb, so I have no idea how long I'll have to wait.

When I flip on the television, I don't recognize any of the channels. All the shows are in Korean. Nothing is in English or even subtitled. They must get a lot of Korean house guests.

I try watching the television shows even though I don't understand them. I kind of like one show where there's this skinny guy with thick-rimmed glasses being taught how to dance by this older muscular guy, only he's really clumsy and goofy and can't get the dance moves right. I'm not sure what they're saying, but the guy with the glasses seems to be saying funny things and still makes me laugh for some reason. Then the muscular guy turns into a head of broccoli and the wacky guy dances around him. A face appears in the corner of the screen, shaped like a cartoon sun, and says something in an angry deep voice as though scolding the guy with the glasses for turning his dance teacher into broccoli. At least, that's all I can make out of it. I'm not sure I would understand this even if I knew how to speak Korean.

I hear nearby voices and turn off the television, thinking it's Spiderweb and her father returning to get me. But when I exit the room, I don't see them anywhere. I listen more carefully. The voices aren't saying anything I can understand. They sound like moans.

Stepping deeper into the house, I follow the moans. Is Spiderweb making the sounds during her operation? No. The moans are deeper, like they're from an older person. I wonder if it's Spiderweb's mother, but the moans come from more than one person. And some of the moans are male.

It sounds like it could come from a television set somewhere. Perhaps a horror movie. Either that or this house is haunted. I'm leaning toward the second option.

I know Spiderweb's family wouldn't like me exploring their house, but I'm too curious about the noises. They are definitely coming from the lower floor, not upstairs where the mother resides. So it can't be Spiderweb's mother or a television show she might be watching.

The sounds come from a dark wing of the building. A hallway with no lights or windows. I tap a light switch, but the lights don't turn on. It's so empty and undecorated that I can't imagine the family regularly goes on this side of the house. Yet this is where the voices come from. A few steps in and I can almost make out four distinct cries. Whoever is making the noises, they must be in incredible pain.

Perhaps they really are ghosts. Perhaps nobody goes on this side of the house because it is haunted.

I take three steps into the darkness, then somebody grabs me from behind.

"Ethan?" Stephen asks.

I turn around to face him.

"Come on," he says. "It's your turn."

I stumble over my words, trying to come up with an excuse for being where I shouldn't have been. "I just... I heard..."

But he doesn't seem to care too much.

"It's dangerous here," Stephen says. "You shouldn't be wandering."

"Dangerous?"

He pulls me out of the darkness. "The family dogs are grumpy these days. They tend to snap at visitors. You should leave them alone."

"They were dogs making those whining noises?" I ask, looking back.

"Whining noises?" he asks. Then he nods. "They do whine a lot."

I could have sworn they were human voices, but perhaps I didn't hear them very clearly. Perhaps they were just dogs whining. I've heard stranger noises come out of dogs in the past.

Stephen leads me into an operating room. It is everything like the ones from the hospital, right down to the funny acrid smell. It's fully supplied with surgery tools and other doctor's equipment. The shelves lined with drugs and chemicals. There's probably not a procedure that couldn't be done in this little room.

"Spiderweb's resting in her room," Stephen says. "She's not used to these operations yet. They take a lot out of her."

Next to the operating table, I notice the bloody tools that Stephen must have used to put his daughter's face back together, as well as a small pile of skin in a green Tupperware container.

"But you don't mind, do you?" he asks. "It'll give us time to get to know each other, just you and me."

I nod, though I have no idea why I'd want to get to know him. I still need to get to know my girlfriend before I get to know her father. He must not be aware of how little we've actually spoken to each other since we started dating.

"Sit up here, Champ," he says, patting the operating chair.

I climb up and he puts a bib around my neck. I feel kind of like I'm at the dentist office. He examines my face carefully. Then nods.

"Yep. Yep. Just as I thought." He lifts a layer of skin and then puts it back down. "You lost a lot of flesh here."

"I did?" I try to get up, but he pushes me back in the seat.

"I'll have to replace it," he says.

My face burns, like it has been split open, but I didn't think I actually lost any skin. I just thought I'd need some stitches at most.

He hands me a mirror and says, "See."

When I see myself, I nearly fall out of the chair in shock. I hadn't seen myself in the mirror before, so I didn't realize how bad my condition really was. Looking at my reflection, it's like half of my face was blown off. Not as bad as Spiderweb's, but I'm clearly missing chunks of flesh from my cheeks and forehead. Even my lips and nose are torn up.

"I don't get it…" I say, touching my wounds. "It doesn't hurt that bad."

Stephen nods. "That would be Spiderweb's doing."

I look up at him with a questioning face.

He says, "She has a natural anesthetic in her blood. The instant her blood mixed with yours, it dulled the pain. You wouldn't have realized the extent of the damage."

"Anesthetic in her blood?" I ask. "How is that possible?"

Stephen doesn't answer right away, organizing his tools and sterilizing his hands with an acidic blue fluid.

When he turns back to me, he says, "Spiderweb is a very special girl, as I'm sure you already know. She comes from a long line of special women."

As he speaks, Stephen cleans my face with the same blue liquid he used on his hands. It burns like rubbing alcohol. I cringe with every drop of fluid that is applied.

"You see," he continues, "Spiderweb, like her mother and grandmother before her, is not like other girls. She

48

is a very passionate person, thousands of times more passionate than a normal human being is capable. When she falls in love, she falls harder than her human body can handle. Love boils up inside her, like a soda shaken in its can. And if her love is strong enough, her human flesh won't be able to contain it for long."

He finishes cleaning my face and says, "She pops," while tapping me once on the center of my forehead. "Then pieces of her go everywhere. I'm sure you found it disgusting at first. I know *I* did the first time Sarah popped in front of me. But once I understood why, I realized it wasn't disgusting at all. It was the most beautiful thing in the world. You see, she only popped because she loved me so much. Sarah was capable of loving someone a thousand times more than any other person could ever love another human being, and she chose me to be the object of her affection. I never felt more special."

Stephen opens a refrigerator and pulls out small trays of human skin. I wonder where all the skin came from. It appears to have been taken from several different donors.

"It's been happening to the women in Spiderweb's bloodline for hundreds, maybe even thousands, of years. They all *pop* whenever they experience strong emotions. Over the generations, their bodies evolved to adapt to the pain of popping. They started growing glands that secrete a unique pain-numbing chemical into their blood at the exact moment they burst."

He shuffles through the pieces of skin on the tray, looking for good matches for my face. "They have also evolved to accept almost any kind of skin tissue. And they heal very quickly. Unfortunately, your wounds will take much longer to heal. Your scars will likely stay with you for the rest of your life. But once Spiderweb has her stitches removed, you'd never have known she was ever wounded."

Stephen stitches the skin to my face as he speaks. His hands are very gentle, weaving through my flesh with a delicate touch. He's probably performed this operation dozens of times before. And with his wife and daughter as patients, it makes sense that he would have learned how to execute the procedure with extreme tenderness and caution.

"It's a special thing to be chosen by a woman of Spiderweb's bloodline," Stephen says. "Not just because they are capable of loving more intensely than normal humans, but because their love is unending. Spiderweb has chosen you as her boyfriend. That means she will love you for the rest of your life. She will be dedicated to you always."

I feel a tugging of flesh as he weaves the needle through my cheek, but can't feel anything else, apart from his breath against my ear as he speaks.

I say, "She really likes me that much? We haven't been dating very long."

Stephen shakes his head. "It doesn't matter how long you've known each other. Once Spiderweb falls in love, she's in love forever. Even if you lose interest in her, she'll still love you. She'll wait for you no matter how long it takes."

Part of me thinks Stephen is just exaggerating. I love

Spiderweb. And I'm glad she loves me, too. But we still barely know each other. There's no way she can already be completely committed to me as he says.

"But it would be a big mistake to reject her love," he continues. "Not only would you be missing out on the greatest love of your life, but it would be terribly selfish to deprive Spiderweb of the only relationship she can possibly have. She can only be with you. If she can't have you she will never have a true relationship."

"Even if I die?" I ask. "What happens to her if I were killed in a car accident or died of a horrible disease?"

He nods at me as he stitches. "Then it would be okay. Her connection lasts for as long as you live, so it would eventually fade away if you were to meet an unfortunate end."

Stephen finishes stitching on a section of my face, cuts the thread, then moves on to another piece of skin. The tone of the flesh is much darker than my own complexion. It's not going to match at all, but I decide not to argue.

"But I hope you never decide to leave my daughter," he says. "If that were to happen then her only chance at happiness would be for you to either change your mind one day or die." His tone gets firm and serious, then he tugs at a thread in my face and says, "I would hate for you to have to die."

It almost sounds like a threat. I'm not sure if he's serious or not. I'm not sure if I even believe anything he's saying about Spiderweb. But I'm pretty sure the man isn't right in the head. I can't imagine what life has been like for my girlfriend to be raised by such strange parents.

When Stephen is done with the operation, he smiles down on me, proud of a job well done. Then he holds up a mirror.

"There you are," he says. "Good as new."

But my face isn't at all as good as new. I look like Spiderweb, like Frankenstein. My face has become a patchwork of different types of skin. I instantly realize what a terrible mistake I made letting Stephen sew me up instead of going to a real doctor.

My eyes widen in the mirror as I feel the new pieces of skin. They're not mine. They're not connected to my nerves. It's like I have pieces of warm leather sewn into my flesh.

"You should be more careful when you're around Spiderweb," Stephen says. "She pops so easily at this age. Before you attempt to kiss her again, you must try to spend as much time with her as possible, get her body used to your presence."

I hand the mirror back to Stephen and say, "So there's a way to prevent it? She won't always explode like that?"

Stephen shakes his head. "She will always pop when her emotions rise. But the more comfortable she is around you, the less frequently it will happen. It requires patience. For now, since having a boyfriend is so new to her, just looking into your eyes for too long can cause her to pop.

Kissing is especially dangerous, for both of you. It would be best if you just focused on spending more time with each other, talking or singing or playing board games. You're welcome to come to our home whenever you wish. We encourage you to visit after school each day, study together, spend much of your free time together. I'm sure you'll quickly become inseparable, as Sarah and I have been for so many years."

My knees wobble as I attempt to stand up on my feet. I feel weak, either from the operation or the drug that was injected into my face. Stephen helps me to the door.

"But there's one thing I need to tell you," Stephen says.

He grabs me by the arm and squeezes tight, not allowing me to take another step.

He says, "It's very important. I can't stress how imperative it is that you heed my words."

His fingers dig into the flesh of my arm, constricting so firmly that I almost cry out. His expression is stern and intense. I'm not sure he even realizes how much strength he's putting into his grip on me.

"Do not," he says. "I repeat: DO NOT."

Then he pauses to take a deep breath. "Under any circumstances…" He grips my arm even tighter. "Try to have sex with my daughter."

His words surprise me. I have no idea what he's talking about. Of course I wouldn't try to have sex with her. We're not even old enough yet.

"Sex with women of Spiderweb's bloodline is a very delicate matter, especially when it's their first time," Stephen continues. "Several precautions must be taken.

53

There is a protocol. It must be supervised."

Stephen is beginning to scare me. The look in his eyes is getting even more intense. I feel like he's about to hit me, physically beat his words into me.

"When you're old enough and feel you're ready, come to me," he says. "Sarah and I will guide you. There's no other way. Please, no matter what you do. Promise me you will not have sex prematurely." Then he shakes my arm violently. "Promise me!"

I gasp at his outburst and cry, "I promise! I won't!"

Then he calms down. "Okay. Good. I'm glad we understand each other."

A smile returns to his face. Then he escorts me out of the operating room.

"Spiderweb will still be resting for another hour or so," Stephen says, walking me down a hallway back toward the foyer. "You should check in on her then. She'll give you a tour of the house. Unfortunately, I must leave you for now. I still have much work to do before I start dinner."

I nod at him and say, "I should call my parents and tell them what happened. Is that okay?"

When I say this, he stops and stares at me in such a way that it seems he's almost offended that I would be interested in contacting my family. It's as though he thinks I should be more concerned with his family than my own. But he quickly shakes the expression away and

54

a smile returns to his face.

"Of course, of course," he says. "But you should wait until later. You don't want to upset your parents while they're still at work, do you? Wait until they get home before letting them know you'll be staying here for dinner."

I nod. I don't really want to stay for dinner and was hoping my parents would have told me I couldn't so that I'd have an excuse to go home, but I'm not sure how to argue with him. I guess I can just wait it out for now.

"You can stay in the Visitor's Center until Spiderweb wakes up," he says.

"Visitor's Center?"

"That's what we call the living room near the entrance."

I nod. I was right when I assumed the room I was in before was some kind of living room for guests. But it's strange they call it a Visitor's Center.

"Do you get a lot of visitors from Korea?" I ask him.

His expression looks surprised. "No... not at all. Why do you ask?"

"The television in there only has Korean television shows."

He laughs and nods his head. "Ah, yes. Spiderweb loves Korean programs. She watches them on that television all the time."

"She speaks Korean?"

"Yes, yes. She speaks Korean fluently, as well as seven other languages. We travel a lot and have lived in many countries. Spiderweb has always been quick at adapting to other tongues, much faster than I have been able to manage. She's a very bright girl."

His statement surprises me. Spiderweb's never seemed to be all that bright of a student in school. I can't believe she knows so many languages. There seems to be so much I don't know about her.

Stephen leaves me in the Visitor's Center and I just stand here for a few minutes, not sure what to do. I would do homework, but all my books are still in my locker at school. There's supposed to be a quiz in science class tomorrow. I hope Mr. Marsh will let me get out of it or else I'll fail. When he looks at my stitched-up face, you'd think he'd understand. But he's usually uninterested in excuses and seems to take pleasure in failing lazy students like myself. I'll have to see how it goes tomorrow.

I watch Korean game shows for a while, not sure how Spiderweb could be so interested in them. She must have developed a taste for these programs while she lived in South Korea. I wonder what the other kids thought of her when she lived there. Was she just as much of an outsider? Being a foreigner, I would think so. Or maybe the people can't tell the difference between a normal foreigner and a weird one, since all foreigners are strange to them. Perhaps she got along better with people there. Perhaps that's why she watches Korean television shows so much. They might remind her of when she was happier and more accepted.

CHAPTER
SIX

After a couple of hours, I decide to go check on Spiderweb. Stephen told me that's what I should do, but he didn't tell me where her room was located. I leave the Visitor's Center and explore the house, hoping I'll be able to figure it out. Most of the doors in the place are closed and locked, so it's not so easy to figure out which rooms are which. I know that it can't be too far from the operating room or else I would have run into her after her surgery.

I return to the hospital wing of the house and explore the nearby rooms one at a time. This area is more decorated than the other parts of the house. It feels more lived in. Paintings line the walls, all of them portraits of women with their husbands and children. Many of them are decades, maybe centuries, old. Most of the adult women in the pictures have patchwork faces, just like Spiderweb's. Some of the husbands are also stitched and scarred. Though there is one photo where the father is the one with patchwork flesh and his wife has no scars at all, as if it is the male who had the exploding disease in this particular generation. Stephen made it seem as though only the females of Spiderweb's bloodline were the ones that suffered from the condition, but perhaps that's not always the case.

Going from room to room, most of the doors here are not locked like the rest of the house. I can tell this must be Spiderweb's wing of the building, because many of the decorations feel like they are of her own design. The doorknobs and door frames have been painted green—her favorite color. Brass sculptures shaped like four leaf clovers are mounted on shelves in the hallway.

I open the doors carefully, knocking twice before entering. The first room I try is a small children's library, filled with books from several different countries. It must be Spiderweb's own private library. Fluffy green couches line the floors, enough sitting space for four or five friends to read together, but only one of the seats seems to have ever been used.

The next room I try is a small office with white and green tables. Notebooks, pens, dictionaries, almanacs and calculators are arranged in neat little piles. It's Spiderweb's private study room. She also has her own dance studio and a toy room filled with dolls and transformers.

I can't believe how rich she is. Never in a million years would I be able to have several rooms to myself. My own library, my own office, my own toy room. It seems insane. I can hardly believe it.

The last room at the end of the hall seems to be Spiderweb's bedroom. It's the only room I haven't checked and it has a portrait of her hung on the outside of the door. The painting must have been created recently, because she's wearing the same outfit she wore on her first date, with the same green makeup and cherry-red pigtails. But it was painted prior to her face exploding, because her skin isn't stitched up in the image. Maybe her parents had it painted for her birthday last month.

I knock on the door twice, but there's no answer. I try again and put my ear to the door. She's either in really deep sleep or I was wrong about this being her bedroom. I turn the knob and open it a crack.

"Jill?" I ask. "Are you in here?"

There is no answer. The room is too dark to see. I open the door wider.

"Jill?"

It is definitely a bedroom. I can see the edges of a large green bed in the dim light. There are thick green curtains hanging from the window, as well as fishnet draperies dangling from the corners of the walls.

I take a step inside. "Hello?"

There is a lump in the bed, but I can't tell if she is actually there. She's not moving.

As I step deeper into the room, something brushes across the top of my head. I rub my hair and feel something sticky between my fingers, something crawling on my hand.

I jump to the light switch and flip it on. It takes a moment for my eyes to adjust, but when they do, what I see makes my pulse quicken. It's just like the rumors say. Hanging from the ceiling, draped over the window and the corners the room, even dangling above the bed—there are dozens of spiders perched on spiral-shaped webs.

There is so much webbing that I can barely see some sections of her room. I can't believe it. I thought it was just a story the other kids made up because of that one time a black widow landed on her in P.E. class. But Jill really does keep spiders for pets. And not even in cages. Their webs are everywhere.

Sleeping in the bed below a massive collection of spider webs that form a white canopy above her, Jill sleeps soundly as though sleeping with spiders was the most normal thing in the world.

"Holy sh—" I look down at the bright red arachnid crawling across my hand and then flick it off.

Examining Jill in her bed, I can't imagine it's safe for her to sleep like that. So many spiders are hanging in the webs above her, any one of them could drop down and land on her as she sleeps. I don't understand how she can be comfortable with this. I can hardly handle standing in the same room with them for a minute, let alone sleeping here.

There's no way I ever would have believed the rumors to be true. She really does have spider friends. She really does let them crawl all over her.

Spiderweb doesn't wake up. I call her name one more time, but she sleeps through it. I decide I better get out of there before another spider lands on me.

But before I leave the room, something catches my attention. On a vanity, behind a curtain of webs, there are dozens of photos that look familiar. Some of them are taped to the mirror, others lined across the counter like collector's cards. Once I recognize the images, I can't believe it. They are pictures of my house.

"What the hell…"

I pull the spider webs apart and take a closer look at the pictures. They aren't just pictures of my house. They are pictures of *me*. Some of them are pictures of me outside my house, some of them are pictures of me in my bedroom, taken through my window. Some of them of me getting ready for school or waiting for the bus at the end of my driveway.

Who took these? Not Spiderweb. They look professional, like they were taken by a photographer. Why would Spiderweb have all of these?

I pick one of them up and examine it carefully. It's a picture of me in my underwear, changing my clothes before bed.

"Ethan?" a voice calls to me from across the room.

I turn to see Spiderweb waking from sleep, staring at me. A smile stretches on her face, excited to see me inside of her creepy room. Then she sees what's in my hands.

"What are these?" I ask.

Her smile turns to a nervous stutter.

I hold up a photo. "Why do you have pictures of me at my home?"

She shakes her head. "It wasn't my fault. My father gave those to me. He thought they'd make me happy."

"Make you happy?"

"So that I could be with you even when we weren't together," she says, sitting up.

She has a nervous, yet innocent look on her face. I think she's telling the truth. I believe her father is the one responsible. He's even stranger than I realized.

"Are you mad?" she asks.

I look down at the photos and shake my head. "It's embarrassing…"

She crawls to the end of the bed in her fuzzy green pajamas. "I'm sorry."

I put them down on her desk. "It's okay. I guess if somebody gave me pictures of you I wouldn't turn them down, even if I felt bad about it."

Her face brightens. "We can do that if you want. You can have pictures of me, to make up for it."

I shake my head at her. For some reason, her proposal seems even creepier. Especially if her father is involved. "It's okay. Just tell him not to do it again."

She nods in agreement, but then looks down with a sulking face, as though disappointed I didn't take her up on the offer to get pictures of her.

As her head lowers, an emerald green garden spider crawls across her hair. When I see it, I jump back and cry out, nearly stumbling into a large collection of webs behind me.

"What?" she asks.

I point at her head. "A spider is in your hair."

"Oh…" She brushes the spider out of her hair and tosses it into a web behind her.

"Why do you have so many spiders in your room?"

She seems embarrassed by it and won't look me in the eyes when she speaks. "I didn't put them in here or anything. Spiders are just attracted to me."

"They're not your pets?" I ask.

She shakes her head. "It's been like this since I was a kid. Spiders always come to me. Mom says it's because there's a scent in my sweat that they like. I used to be scared of them and think they were creepy and I'd kill them. But now I've gotten used to it, so I just let them build their webs around me. It's easier than trying to clean them out every day."

"Don't they bite you?" I ask.

She shakes her head. "Spiders don't usually bite people. They're actually very gentle, as long as you remain calm around them and don't try to squish them."

"Is it because of your bloodline? Are spiders also attracted to your mother?"

"Yeah, but it's different for everyone. I attract spiders. My mother attracts bees. They used to call her Beehive when she was a kid, like they call me Spiderweb."

I nod, then smile. It's just dawned on me that I've had a whole conversation with Spiderweb and I never hesitated once. Even though it was a strange conversation, neither of us were too shy to speak. And her face didn't even explode.

When I look her in the eyes, I realize she's thinking the exact same thing I am. She smiles at me.

Then she says, "I need to get dressed."

I nod. "Okay."

She gets out of the bed and opens her dresser. "You can stay if you want, just look the other way."

"No, no…" My face turns red. "It's okay. I'll meet you in the Visitor's Center."

She nods at me and says. "Okay. I won't be too long."

Before I leave the room, I look back and catch her staring at me. She doesn't say anything. She just stares.

"What?" I ask.

She smiles and diverts her eyes. "Sorry…"

Then she says, "It's just… our faces match now. We're the same." She points at my stitched together face. "We're perfect for each other."

CHAPTER
SEVEN

On the way back to the Visitor's Center, a howling sound echoes through the house. I stop in my tracks. The sound continues. It must be the family dogs Stephen was talking about.

But as I pass the dark wing of the building, I listen more carefully. The howling doesn't sound animal. It sounds human. Like a man crying out in pain. Could they really be dogs, or was Spiderweb's father lying to me?

Then I hear what distinctly sounds like a woman's voice crying for help. I'm convinced. There has to be people down there. But I don't understand why.

I step into the dark hallway. Spiderweb's father does seem like a psychopath. I wouldn't put it past him to keep people locked in his basement. Prisoners he keeps for God knows what purpose.

Then it dawns on me: the skin. Both Spiderweb and her mother need skin donors to replace the flesh they lose when they pop. Is it possible that they aren't volunteer donors? Is it possible that Stephen kidnaps people and locks them in his basement, keeping them as a source of skin for his wife and daughter?

I have to help them. I have to call the police and get them rescued. But what if I'm wrong? What if they really are just dogs that make human-like sounds?

I decide I have to check it out. I have to see them with my own eyes. If they are dogs then I'll be able to rest easy. If they are prisoners then I'll call for help. But I have to move quickly, before Stephen or Spiderweb know where I've gone.

Spiderweb should be done changing any minute, so I don't have much time. I rush to the end of the hallway, feeling my way through the dark, following the howling sounds.

The door at the end is locked, but the key is still in the doorknob. I pray there are only dogs on the other side. If they are people, I don't know what I'm going to do. I'll have to figure out how to call for help without letting Spiderweb or her parents know that I've discovered their secret. But I have to be careful. If they catch me in the act they might lock me down in the basement with the other prisoners. They might never let me leave.

When I open the door, the howling stops. I feel the wall for a light switch.

"Hello?" I call out. "Is anyone there?"

I find the light switch and flip it on. A small dangling light bulb illuminates in front of me, brightening a staircase leading down into a deep hole in the ground. The cellar wasn't originally a part of the house. Somebody dug it out. The steps leading down are made of two-by-fours, cut into yard-long pieces and nailed together, probably crafted by hand.

"Is anyone down there?" I call into the darkness below.

I hear someone whimpering. It sounds like a woman's voice. She doesn't respond.

"Are you okay?"

The steps don't feel very sturdy, so I take them slow, one at a time. When I get to the bottom, I realize the basement is more of a cave system than a cellar. The floor and walls are just rock and dirt. The light from the top of the stairs only brightens a small section of the underground, leaving the majority of it covered in shadow.

The whimpers come from the left of me. But there are other noises far to my right. This underground cave system must be as large as the entire house, or maybe larger, maybe their entire property. I don't have time to search it all. I just need to see if I'm right about the people being kept down here.

I see movement. The whimpering sound grows louder.

"Hello?" I ask.

As my eyes adjust to the darkness, I see a human figure. A woman's arms and legs. But not her whole body.

"Are you alright?" I call out.

Then the figure stops whimpering and turns toward me. She's not chained up as I originally expected. She barks and charges me. I now realize I've made a horrible mistake coming down into this basement.

"What the fuck!" I cry out.

As she crawls into the light, I get a good look at her. It's not a woman, nor a dog. It's something else. Some kind of massive creature. She's naked and covered in dirt and scabby wounds. Three times the size of a normal woman, with two pairs of tree trunk-sized arms, a long slender snake-like torso, and short stump-like legs. A tiny girl's face centers a large bulbous head, yelping and howling as she comes at me.

I turn to run but the thing is far too fast. She jumps at me and knocks me to the ground. Looking into her small black eyes as she opens her mouth filled with jagged teeth, I assume she's going to rip my throat out right there. But she doesn't hurt me. She sticks out her tongue and licks me from my neck up to my forehead. Then she pants in my face, her tongue dangling out. A hot rotten flesh smell spills from her maw.

Three more similarly-deformed creatures come out of the dark and lick my face. I cringe and try to push them back. They aren't trying to hurt me. They're absolutely disgusting, but friendly. Still, after being held down and licked by them for a minute, I can't take it anymore. I scream and push them away. Run up the stairs and leave the cellar. They're too big to make it up the steps after me.

Before I close the basement door, Spiderweb catches me in the act. She sees me gasping in a panic, covered in dirt and foul saliva.

"Did you go down there?" she asks, coming toward me. "You're not supposed to go down there."

She's wearing a pretty new dress and a fresh coating of green makeup, as though trying to make herself look nice for me. I don't know what to do. I just run past her.

"I need to go home," I say, heading for the exit.

Spiderweb runs after me.

"You can't leave," she says. "You have to stay for dinner."

But I'm too freaked out to spend another minute in this house.

I shake my head and continue. "No, I have to go. I'm sorry."

"At least let Daddy drive you home."

I don't listen to her. I run out the front door and charge down the driveway. It'll be at least an hour of walking to get home, but I don't care. I need to get far away from that place. And I don't plan on ever going back.

CHAPTER
EIGHT

I want to ditch school today. I'm afraid to face Spiderweb for running out on her yesterday. But my parents wouldn't let me. They're mad at me and forced me to go. They spent all night yelling at me for having a strange man stitch me up instead of going to a real hospital. They were going to call the police. I had to beg them not to. I didn't know what Spiderweb's father would do to me if I got him into trouble.

When Spiderweb comes onto the bus, I don't look at her. I leave my backpack on the seat next to me, hoping she'll take the hint and sit somewhere else. But she just moves the backpack and sits down anyway.

"You shouldn't have left so suddenly," she says. "My parents were really worried about you."

I don't look at her, staring out the window. I rub the stitches on my face. My wounds are itchy and swollen and hurt. Spiderweb notices my agony. She digs into her backpack.

"Daddy wanted you to have these," she says.

I look down at a small bottle of pills in her hand.

"They're for the pain," she says. "Take one every four hours."

Although I want to just ignore her, I don't think I'll be able to handle the pain for much longer. I grab the bottle from her hand and take a dose, but I still don't say anything.

We sit in silence for a while. A few bus stops later, she says, "You shouldn't have gone into the basement. You weren't ready to see our dogs."

I quiver at the memory. "Those weren't dogs."

"I know they look strange, but they're just animals," she says. "My family has been breeding them for generations."

I look at her for a second, then look away.

"They look like giant people," I say.

She grabs my hand, tries to get me to look into her eyes. "They have the same DNA as people, but they're not really people. They have the intelligence of dogs. We can't get skin from donors and don't want to take it against a person's will. This is the best solution we have. And it has worked for a hundred generations."

I don't know what to say. It's so horrifying that they keep those things under their house. And to think that the skin on my face, the skin on Spiderweb's face, comes from those creatures they breed underground. It absolutely disgusts me.

But the more I think about it, the more it makes sense. They don't have any other choice. And I shouldn't take it out on Spiderweb. It's not her fault for being born into such a grotesque family.

"You don't want to break up with me, do you?" she

71

asks. "My parents really liked you..."

I don't answer her right away, thinking about it. Although there are so many strange things about her and her family, I can't imagine being with anyone but her. I wish she was more like a normal girl, but I'd rather be with her and deal with her eccentricities than never see her again. Besides, if what her father says is true, she can't love anyone else but me. If I reject her now I'll be condemning her to a life of loneliness.

"Of course I don't want to break up with you," I tell her.

When I say this, her face brightens into a smile. She squeezes my hand and presses her stitched-up face against mine.

The ordeal yesterday was traumatic for me, but it seems to have brought us closer together. We can talk to each other without anxiety. She can get close to me without exploding. If I can just get over what her life is like at home I know we'll have a beautiful future together.

At school, the other kids are terrified of us as we walk down the hallways toward class, walking hand in hand as a real couple for the first time. They see that my face is just as stitched up as Spiderweb's. Their jaws drop, stepping out of our path as we walk. I can sense what they're thinking. They see us as Frankenstein and Frankenstein's Bride, for real this time, and I couldn't be happier about it. Their fear only makes me giggle.

When we get to our homeroom classes, ready to separate, I tell her, "See you at lunch."

Then I kiss her. I do it quickly, before she expects it so that her face doesn't explode. She doesn't move, just staring at me with a smile on her face in the middle of the hallway as I go inside my homeroom.

The other kids are too scared to even look at me for more than a second in class. Even Josh is terrified of me. He switches seats, moving to the back of the room, frightened of being too close. The others near me inch their desks away from me a little at a time, trying to stay as far away as possible.

For the entire period, I'm unable to stop snickering to myself. I realize that I'm finally safe. People won't pick on me anymore. They're just as scared of me as they are of Spiderweb. It's like they thought of Spiderweb as a vampire who has turned me into one of her own kind. I'm sure they'll all talk about me behind my back, but they won't confront me like they used to. I can finally date Spiderweb without worry of ridicule and bullying.

The second I see Big Mark Henney in the bathroom before lunch, I realize that I was wrong to believe I was completely safe. He's been waiting for me, ready to finish what he started yesterday. When he sees my face, it only fazes him for a second. He must not have heard about

73

my new Frankenstein skin yet. But he tries to stay tough, not let my appearance frighten him. Freaks don't scare him as much they scare the other students. With those weird tumor-like growths on his belly, he's still a bigger freak than I am.

"What's with your face?" he says. "Stick it in your girlfriend's crotch for too long?"

I try not to act intimidated. I'm done with being bullied. Now is the time I let him know that he can't push me around anymore.

"I don't get it," I say, walking casually into one of the stalls to take a piss. "What's that supposed to mean?"

Although I'm trying to be brave, I still use the stall to go to the bathroom. I know better than to use the urinal. Mark Henney is known to kick people at the urinal, causing them to pee all over themselves.

"It means you got an STD from licking her diseased vagina," he says, as I close the stall door in his face. "And the STD turned you into a Frankenstein just like her." Then he jumps up and grabs the door, pulling himself up so that he can look at me in the stall. "Get it now?"

I glare up at him and say, "Word of advice, Mark: jokes aren't funny if you have to explain them."

He gives me an angry face and says, "It wasn't a joke," with as much venom as he can muster. But I can't take him seriously as he struggles to stay hanging from the stall door. At fifteen years old, he's a large guy, but he's not the most athletic kid in the eighth grade. Before he can say anything else, he loses his grip and drops back to his feet.

"Yeah, I noticed," I say.

I'm not very good with comebacks, especially when I'm nervous. But my response is enough to make the bully feel stupid. And there's nothing that angers Mark more than being made to feel stupid.

He kicks the stall door, trying to intimidate me. I find it difficult to urinate with him outside the door, but I try to anyway. I'm not going to let him win. Five minutes pass and I still can't get myself to pee even though my bladder is ready to burst. Mark peeks through the crack in the door and snickers at me.

"You think you can hide in there forever?" he asks. "I don't care. I'll wait. It's Sloppy Joe day and I fucking hate Sloppy Joes, so I'm not in any rush."

Eventually, I'm able to piss. And once it starts, nothing Mark does can disrupt me.

"You peeing sitting down in there?" he asks, even though he can see me standing through the door crack. "I knew it. You have a vagina, don't you?"

Being bullied through a stall door is beginning to feel ridiculous. I can't help but laugh, despite the nervousness of what's likely to happen once I open the door. My hands won't stop shaking as I zip up my pants.

"So what if I do have a vagina?"

It's the only comeback I can think of.

He responds, "Then I'll shove my fist up it."

I flush the toilet and exhale deeply to calm myself. I casually step out of the stall and head for the sink. Mark gets in my path, but all I have to do is hold my unwashed hands up to his face to get him to back away. It's funny a tough guy like him would be scared off by a few germs.

As I wash my hands, Mark hovers over me. He leans in to my ear and whispers, "You're such a little faggot, you know that?"

I shrug, trying to remain unfazed.

"How am I a faggot?" I ask. "I have a girlfriend."

"Yeah, but I bet your girlfriend has a dick. She probably fucks you with it in your vagina."

I dry my hands with a brown paper towel. "If she has a dick and I have a vagina, then that doesn't make me a faggot. It makes me a woman in a straight relationship."

"It makes you a she-male who fucks a dude," he says.

I shrug. Then I crumple up the paper towel, throw it in the trash, and say, "If you say so."

As I turn away, Mark grabs me by the arm and pulls me toward him. "I *do* say so. I think you're gay and I think you want to suck my wobblies."

As he holds me close to him, I notice his deformed lumps swelling under his shirt. I struggle to get away from him, but he tightens his grip.

"I'm sure you'd love that," I say, trying to act tough. But my heart is beating so hard he can probably hear it.

Mark lifts his shirt and points the red tumors in my direction. "Not as much as you."

I wiggle out of his grip and back away from him.

"Leave me alone," I say. "If you want a guy to suck your weird stomach dicks, then come out of the closet and get a boyfriend already."

He just stares at me, holding his shirt up, grinding his teeth.

"That is why you're obsessed with me, isn't it? You're hoping I'm really into guys like you are. Sorry, it's not going to happen."

He continues his stare, his eyes burning with frustration. Despite his homoerotic method of bullying, I don't think he's actually gay, at least not completely. That would be too easy. No, Mark is just an asshole who wants to hurt people psychologically as well as physically. I have to show him that no matter what he says or does, he can't get to me. Emotionally, I'm stronger than he is. After what happened to me at Spiderweb's house yesterday, there's nothing he can do that will torment me.

"It's okay," I tell him. "I'm not homophobic. Your secret's safe with me." I fake-smile at him, using a fake-friendly tone. "Maybe I can even help you find a boyfriend."

Mark is pissed. Not because my words insult him. He's just pissed that things aren't going as he planned.

All he says is, "You're dead."

Then he punches me in the face.

The second his fist makes contact, I regret attempting to act tough in front of the guy. Mark is twice my size. Pissing him off only makes him hit harder.

His knuckles feel like cinder blocks against my cheek. My head twists back. My brain jiggles in my skull. And then I feel the stitches break open, the sound of tearing flesh echoes through the bathroom.

I fall back, a sheet of skin dangling from my cheek. When I look back at Mark, his eyes are wide with shock, his mouth drooped open. I turn to my reflection in the mirror. The new skin hangs from the side of my face, exposing my cheekbone.

"You motherfucker…" I say to him, while looking at the damage he did to my face.

I glare at him. He looks terrified.

"I didn't mean to…" he says.

I don't know if it's the adrenaline rushing through my body or because Mark appears weak and afraid, but I flip out. I charge him. He turns to run, but I jump at his legs and tackle him to the floor. My fists aren't bricks like his, but I punch him with all my strength. I hit him in the kidneys, then in the back of his head.

"I'm sorry," he cries. "Get off of me."

I reach around his waist and grab one of his disgusting growths and squeeze as hard as I can. He screams. Then I rip it off. I don't even realize what I'm doing until blood sprays across the tile floor. The strange red tumor pulses in my fingers.

The second Mark sees it in my hand, he changes. Just as I did when I saw my damaged face, he flips out. He throws me off of him and gets to his feet. Before I can get up, he kicks me in the face. The flap of skin is torn off, sticking to the side of his tennis shoe like a wad of wet toilet paper. Then he stomps down on my stomach and kicks me in the waist, blood leaking down his shirt. I grab his leg before he can kick me again and bite into his ankle until a small chunk of flesh comes off in my mouth.

Other kids hear the commotion and rush into the bathroom, slipping on our blood. Josh is among them. He stares at me in horror, seeing a piece of my face on

Mark's shoe, a chunk of his flesh dangling from my lips. We probably look like two rabid dogs going at each other. But we don't stop.

I grab another tumor beneath his shirt. He punches me in the face, ripping away more sections of skin, but I don't let go. I pull with all my strength until it tears off into my hand. Then he howls in pain as he stomps on my head, breaking my nose.

"Holy shit…" someone says. I think it's the fat kid, Tony.

After another kick, I don't have the strength to fight back any more. My rage fades and the pain flows in. I cover my face as he pummels me, trying not to lose anymore facial skin. But Mark doesn't stop. He only gets angrier with every attack, aiming for my neck and skull, like he's actually trying to kill me.

Then I hear a girl's scream barreling toward us. It's Spiderweb. She must have just entered the bathroom and saw what he was doing to me, and freaked out.

She grabs Mark from behind and jumps on his back, shrieking in his ear, "Get off him!"

Mark tries to push her away, but she digs her nails into his neck, bites at his ear, and uses her weight to pull him to the ground.

"Fucking psycho freak!" he yells at her.

Before I know what's going on, I feel something in my pants. I look down. Spiderweb's hand is inside of my underwear, caressing my penis. Everyone in the room sees it, wondering what the hell she is doing. She grabs my hand and pulls it under her shirt, wrapping

79

my fingers around her tiny breast.

I have no idea why she's doing this until I see her face bubbling.

"Don't!" I yell.

But she doesn't listen to me. She presses her face against Mark's temple just as the boiling rises to a climax.

The kids scream as Spiderweb's face explodes. It's bigger than all the other times I've seen, three times as powerful. Mark Henney's entire skull splinters into pulp and sprays across the bathroom wall. His headless body sways in Spiderweb's arms until she lets him go and he plops to the ground with a wet thud.

Once Spiderweb turns her head and shows the other kids her faceless skull as she hovers over Mark's corpse, they all run out of the bathroom, screaming in horror. Still weak and dizzy from the beating I took, Spiderweb helps me to my feet.

"Come on," she says. "We have to get out of here."

I just nod and follow her out of the bathroom. Everyone sees us with our bloody fleshless faces as we flee from the school. None of them seem to care that we're injured or try to help us, they just crumple in fear like we're the dead brought back to life. Not even the teachers stop us as we stagger past them, leaving a trail of blood across the tile floor.

Once we get far enough away, Spiderweb calls her father

and has him pick us up. She tells him everything that's happened and then he tells us to meet him behind the grocery store a few blocks away.

We get there first, so we hide in the bushes and wait for him.

"Don't worry," Spiderweb says. "Daddy will fix this. He'll make everything right."

"You killed him..." I say, as the reality of what had just happened sinks in. "Mark's dead..."

She squeezes my hand. "I didn't have a choice. He was hurting you. I'll kill anyone who tries to hurt you."

Then she rubs her blood into my face. At first, I don't know what the hell she's doing, until all my pain fades away. I allow her to continue applying her blood to my wounds, but try not to look at her gory skinless face as she does it.

A gray van with tinted windows pulls up near us and Stephen steps out. We leave the bushes. Spiderweb runs to him, hugs him tightly, pressing her bloody skull against his shoulder.

"It's okay, it's okay..." he says to her, rubbing her shoulder.

I don't approach them, too nervous to get close to Stephen. I have no idea what he's capable of. He might even blame me for what happened. It might have been better to deal with the police than to deal with him. Stephen speaks to his daughter for a few minutes, but I don't know what they're saying. When they finish, they both look at me. Stephen has a very serious look on his face.

Spiderweb stays with the van as her father approaches me.

"Ethan?" He holds out his hands, taking cautious steps, as though worried I might panic and flee. "How are you feeling? Are you okay?"

I can't speak. I just stare at him.

"I'm sorry this is so sudden, but I need to ask you something." He gets down on one knee and looks me in the eyes. "Will you marry my daughter?"

His question throws me back. I wasn't expecting him to say that at all. And he says it in such a disturbing tone, kneeling like he's proposing to me himself.

"What?" I say.

He breaks into a nervous laugh and says, "I know, I know. You're only thirteen. It's far too huge of a decision for you to make at your age, with no time to even think about it. But it's now or never." He looks back at his daughter, then back at me. "After what happened, we can't stay here. We have to go away and we'll never come back. If you want to have a future with my daughter you have to come with us. Otherwise, you'll never see her again."

"But can't you explain to the police what happened?" I ask. "She was protecting me. Mark might have killed me if she hadn't done it."

Stephen shakes his head. "We can't speak to the police. We can't allow anyone to know about Spiderweb, what she is. They'll lock her away forever. They'll lock her mother away. There's no discussing it. We're leaving now and you're either coming with us or you're not."

"I don't want Spiderweb to leave…" I say.

He shakes his head. "She *has* to leave, but you can come with her if you want. You can get married. You can be with her forever. But if you decide to come with us, you too can never return. You will have to move far away. You will get a new name, a new identity. You will never see your friends or family again."

"You want me to leave my family? I can't see them ever again?"

He takes a deep breath and then exhales. "You won't even get a chance to say goodbye."

I look down. I can't believe what he's asking. I love Spiderweb, but leaving my family?

"I'm sorry," he says. "But we don't have time for you to think it over. We must leave now. What will it be? Will you stay or will you marry my daughter?"

I look at him, then I look at Spiderweb. She is standing there, holding her breath with anticipation. Even with her skinless face, I can still see her excited expression beaming at me. I can't help but smile.

The idea of losing my family terrifies me. The idea of leaving with Spiderweb and her parents terrifies me even more. But I can't lose her. Not now.

I nod my head. "Okay."

"So you agree?" Stephen asks, a smile creeping on his lips.

"Yes. I'll marry her."

Then Spiderweb runs at me and wraps her arms around me, kissing my neck with sticky blood-filled kisses. If she had any flesh left on her face I'm sure it would explode all over me.

As we head toward the van, I see Stephen putting a hypodermic needle into his pocket. My smile fades from my face when I see it. I'm not sure what is in the needle, but whatever it is I bet he planned to inject it into me if I gave him the wrong answer. It's either a sedative that would have knocked me out, forcing me to go with them against my will. Or it's a lethal injection, intended to kill me so that Spiderweb would be able to fall in love with another boy after moving away.

I decide to forget that I saw the needle. I chose to go with Spiderweb, so it doesn't matter what would have happened to me if I had chosen otherwise. I made a decision and I plan to stick with it. There's no going back now.

CHAPTER
NINE

We move across the country. We don't take much. Just a few bags. Everything else is left in the hands of a small army of movers in black suits. They even take the mutant dog creatures that live in the caves below the house. I don't ask who the movers are or where they came from. They seem like the types who are paid not to ask questions.

The new house is fully furnished by the time we arrive. It feels as though it had already been there, waiting for Spiderweb's family to move in. Perhaps they own houses all over the place that are just sitting around in case they need a new place to flee to in a hurry. They seem like they can afford it.

We change our last name to Bryant. My name becomes Evan. Jill becomes Jane. Stephen becomes William. Sarah becomes Susan. Although I'm supposed to become Spiderweb's husband, for now I'm to pretend to be her brother. And I must pretend that her parents are my parents.

It's all very awkward at first, trying to live a new life with a new family. Once we start school together, pretending to be brother and sister yet still acting as boyfriend and girlfriend, it's even more awkward. Spiderweb holds my hand in the hallways and kisses me before class. Everyone thinks we're some kind of scary incest family with horrific patchwork faces. But I try not to care what any of them think. Spiderweb and I are in our own private world. Nobody else matters to us.

One good thing about being a part of Spiderweb's family is that I get my own wing of the house. I can hide away from the rest of the family if I want, spend time by myself. In addition to my own bedroom with a giant king-sized bed, I also have my own living room, my own video game room, my own library and study room. My wing of the house is even larger than Spiderweb's. I think they gave me such special treatment as a way of welcoming me to their family. Perhaps even to make up for being forced to leave my parents as I did.

I miss my parents, but not as much as I thought I would. It feels more like I've gone on a trip without them, like spending a month at summer camp as I used to do every year. I'm sure I will see them again eventually. I hope they're not too worried about me. I wonder if they think I'm dead.

Spiderweb loves having me around. We spend most of our time together, study together, watch television together. Even when I'm playing video games in my video game room, she'll sit behind me and watch me play, even though she has no interest in games. Likewise, I'll often sit with her when she watches Korean television shows, even though I have no idea what anyone is saying.

Her face has only exploded three times since we've lived together. We're usually able to kiss without incident and can stop in time if her face starts to bubble. But a couple of times we made out for a little too long, got a little too carried away. The third time her face exploded, we weren't even kissing. We were just sitting together doing homework when her face popped all over the papers. She says it was just because she was thinking about how much she loved me, how happy she was having me around.

Stephen, or William as he is called now, is not as scary as I thought he would be. He's actually kind of the nicest guy I've ever met. We play pool, foosball and air hockey in the family billiard hall on Fridays, just him and me. We also sometimes throw a baseball around in the massive five acres of forest they call their backyard. He buys me anything I want, whenever I want. And most days he lets me choose what we have for dinner. Even if it's pizza and ice cream three nights in a row. He always tells me that he's happy to have me around, that he's really starting to see me as a son. But I don't know if I'll ever be able to see him as a father.

It is not the same way with Susan, Spiderweb's mother. Although William tells me about how much she loves me and how happy she is that I'm with them now, she doesn't seem to like me very much. She doesn't ever speak to me. She always flees the room whenever I enter. She doesn't eat dinner with the rest of the family. William says she's shy. She hasn't spent much time with people other than her daughter and husband for many years.

She's never had a job or much of a social life. She's a very private person. I'm fine with it, though. I'd prefer not to be around her much. Her appearance still frightens me.

I don't go into Spiderweb's bedroom very often. After just a few weeks of moving into the new house, she already attracted dozens of spiders who built webs in the corners of her room. After living with her for a while, I understand that it really is something in her sweat that attracts the spiders. Not just her bedroom, but any place that she's been will attract them. If she studies at a desk for an afternoon, the next day there will be a spider spinning a web across the back of the chair. If she lies on a couch, watching a television show marathon over a weekend, the couch will soon become home to several crawling arachnids.

At first, I was worried about her spending too much time in my wing of the building. I wanted my side of the house to be spider-free. I even used to spray down any chair or couch she sat in on my side of the house, to kill the odor she leaves behind. But I gave up eventually. I've had so many spiders crawling on me while being with her, that I realized they were too difficult to avoid. A brown recluse once crawled across my shoulder as I hugged her goodnight. I found a yellow sac spider dangling from my lip after making out with her for half an hour. A wolf spider carrying dozens of babies on its back once crawled across our laps while watching television on the couch together.

I've had so many arachnids crawl on me since I've been living with Spiderweb, that they don't freak me out so much. I just make sure they stay out of my room. I can't handle the thought of spiders crawling on me while I sleep. Any spider caught in my bedroom after dark gets squished without mercy.

But it makes me wonder what it will be like once we're married and share the same bedroom. Spiderweb says that we will when that day comes, but I don't know if I'll be able to handle it. William and Susan don't share the same bedroom. I've seen Susan's bedroom once. The place is horrific. There are bees everywhere. The walls are covered in honeycomb, like her room has become one giant beehive. She even sleeps while coated in bees, like the insects form a warm buzzing blanket around her. William says he wishes he could share a room with her, but he can't go into her hive for very long without getting stung. He says he's probably been stung five thousand times since he's known his wife. But he also says that it's all been worth it. I really hope I do not have to suffer through five thousand spider bites by the time I'm his age.

I sometimes hear the strange creatures that live beneath the house, but I don't dare go down there to see them. I still have nightmares about those things. I'd prefer if I never saw them again. Sometimes Spiderweb goes down there to play with them. She says they're actually really tame and friendly, despite their grotesque size and appearance. She usually talks about them just like they were normal dogs.

William is the only person who goes down to visit the creatures on a regular basis. He goes down twice a day. Once to feed them. Once to clean up their shit. And every once in a while he goes down to harvest pieces of their skin. But he doesn't seem very comfortable with the creatures. Since he wasn't born into this family, he probably was once as horrified by the mutants as I am now. They are probably difficult things to get used to, unless you've known them your whole life like Spiderweb and her mother.

The more time I spend with Spiderweb's family, the more I realize how lonely they are. They don't associate with anyone outside of their home. None of them have day jobs. They come from old money and are so rich that they'll never have to worry about working for another twelve generations. So they have plenty of time on their hands. The strange thing is, however, they don't seem to spend much of their time together. They all have their own wings of the house. Each of them stay to their own. Spiderweb tells me about how she spent most of her childhood in her rooms, playing by herself. She would only see her father during dinner and then a few times throughout the week. And she often wouldn't see her mother for days at a time. She rarely ever saw her parents together.

"Let's never be like that," I tell her.

And she nods in agreement.

Sometimes I see William sitting by himself on one of

the upstairs balconies, drinking from a bottle of bourbon. When I see him drinking, I usually don't go anywhere near him. Before my mother quit drinking, she used to get angry when she drank. It taught me to steer clear of adults holding liquor bottles. But one time I decide to say hi to William while he's drinking. He doesn't respond. I go over to him anyway, sit down on the bench next to him, and look out at their lush green property.

Then he goes on to tell me about how much he loves Susan, or Sarah, or whatever her name was when they first met. He says she used to pop for him so much. Every time they would kiss, every time she would look him in the eyes. She used to explode at the drop of a hat. Because she loved him so much.

He takes a swig of whiskey and then tells me all about how much he wishes she would pop for him the way she used to. He says her face hasn't exploded in over a decade, not since Spiderweb was born. He tells me about how much he misses it. He tells me he wishes she would again, just once, so that he would feel as special as he did when they first met.

At first, it sounds like their love is fading. But I thought that was impossible. When he first told me about Spiderweb's bloodline, he said that the women love their men forever and ever, and never love anyone else again for as long as they live. How can she not pop for him if she still loves him so much?

He tells me that she does still love him with all her heart, but she's grown so used to him that her face no longer explodes, no matter how intimate they get. She's grown too familiar with him. But I don't understand what his problem is. The less Spiderweb explodes, the better our relationship has been. We can be as close to each other as we want. We can even kiss for extended periods of time. I sometimes pray that she never explodes again. But here William is, completely depressed over it. I don't understand.

"You will understand, someday," he tells me. "Once your relationship loses its explosiveness, it won't ever be the same."

Before I leave him, William tells me that the next time Spiderweb's face explodes, I'll have to be the one who sews her up.

"Are you kidding?" I ask him.

"You have to learn sooner or later," he says. "It is one of the many skills you are required to master as a husband of the bloodline."

CHAPTER
TEN

As time passes, Spiderweb and I only become closer. We're almost always together, wrapped around each other's bodies, kissing each other with patchwork lips. We find it difficult to be apart. Although we're supposed to be brother and sister, we can't stand the idea of having a platonic relationship at school. We're always all over each other wherever we go.

Although Spiderweb doesn't care or even notice what other people say about us, I still suffer from the occasional embarrassment. Whenever people ask me why I'm making out with my sister all the time, I tell them that she's not my real sister. We're not related by blood. Her family adopted me a few years ago and we started dating soon after that. Whenever I tell this story, they are more understanding about our relationship. They don't think it's quite as weird. But they still don't think of it as exactly normal.

By our third year of high school, Spiderweb has stopped exploding around me. We've been together for so long and are so comfortable with each other, that it seems weird to not be holding each other most of the time. Now, no matter what we do, her face remains intact.

Without the explosions, Spiderweb's face has healed perfectly. She doesn't look Frankenstein-ish at all anymore. She looks more beautiful than ever before, more beautiful than any girl in the whole school. Her face is still a collection of different colors of skin, but it only makes her look more unique, more fascinating to admire. Even her mismatched eyeballs are strangely alluring.

I, on the other hand, have not healed quite so nicely. My face is riddled with scars, my skin bulbous and rough-textured. I constantly look as though I've been run over by a tractor. But Spiderweb still loves me no matter how scarred my face. She doesn't even look at other guys, despite the attention she's been getting from them lately. In her world, only I exist.

Because Spiderweb hasn't been exploding on me, we've been able to get more intimate than we used to be able to. In my video game room back home, sometimes she'll take her bra off and let me suck on her puffy white nipples. Sometimes she'll rub my penis between her pale, freckled fingers. She wants us to start having sex. She thinks it's time. But I always refuse her. I'll never forget her father's warning that I shouldn't have sex without coming to him first. He said the act would need to be supervised.

"He's just being overprotective," she says. "Do you really want to do it with him watching?"

I shake my head. That's the last thing I'd want. "I at least want to talk to him about it, just to understand why."

"It's bullshit," she says, making sure I see her breasts bursting out of the top of her green striped shirt. "He'll just ruin it."

But I don't give in. She's been trying to seduce me into it for days, but I'm just too worried.

"I haven't popped in almost a year," she says. "It'll be safe. I don't get overwhelmed anymore. Sex won't be any different."

"But what if you get pregnant?" I ask.

She shrugs. "That's okay. I want to get pregnant soon anyway."

"You want to get pregnant soon? We're only seventeen."

"But we've been married for four years already. I want to start having sex. I want to start having babies."

"We're not officially married yet. Not until after high school."

"That's just when we can finally have the ceremony. The day you ran away with me was the day we got married. That's how I'll always see it."

"In any case, we should wait," I tell her.

"Until when?" she asks.

I shrug. "We should just wait."

But it's easy for me to say. I masturbate regularly, so I'm able to release sexual tension whenever I want to. It's not the same way with Spiderweb. She's never masturbated in her life. Something about her bloodline won't let her. Sex means nothing to her unless her chosen mate is involved. She's not aroused by anyone or anything else. So masturbation does nothing for her. It's either sex with me or continued sexual frustration.

Spiderweb has been sneaking into my bedroom at night and crawling into bed with me. She doesn't care that it's against her father's rules. He doesn't ever come to our side of the house anyway.

She squeezes under the covers, wraps her arms around me, and sleeps with her body pressed against mine. Even though she leaves her scent all over my bed, attracting all sorts of spiders into my room, I don't ever tell her to go. These are my favorite times I spend with her. These are the moments that reassure me that choosing a life with Spiderweb was the right decision, even though I had to leave my family and old life behind.

I still miss my parents. I sometimes cry alone in my bedroom when I think about them. But I would never trade Spiderweb to get them back. I just feel bad that they have no idea what happened to me. I wish they knew that I'm safe and happy. I wish they could meet Spiderweb and attend our wedding next year.

But these thoughts vanish as Spiderweb curls around me beneath the covers. We fall asleep with our limbs entwined, our breath tickling each other's faces.

In the middle of the night, I awake to her scrupulous gaze. We are within a large spider web that has been built around us overnight, cocooning us together. She doesn't say anything, just stares at me. She isn't wearing any clothing. I soon realize that neither am I. She must have taken off my pajamas while I slept. Her naked skin is warm and smooth against mine. The spider web above us glistens in the moonlight shining through the windows.

"Kiss me," she says.

I press my lips to hers. It makes me remember the first time we kissed, back in the eighth grade, when we barely knew each other. Her face doesn't pop when I kiss her this time, but the emotions we feel are no less explosive.

We wrap our arms around each other and our kiss deepens, her breasts pushing into my chest. I've never been fully naked with her before. We've touched each other's privates, made out with our shirts off, but never completely naked, never while in bed together. It feels new. Every inch of my skin is sensitive to her touch.

"Go down on me," she says, pushing me under the covers.

I do as she says, but move with caution. I've never given her oral sex before, not sure what would happen if I did. Anything new is dangerous with Spiderweb. I have no idea what will set her off. I've grown so fond of her face being in one piece that I'd hate to see it explode again.

She grips the sheets tightly as I lick her. I'm not sure exactly what to do, so I just explore her with my tongue, paying close attention to what makes her respond. But since she's been building up to this moment for so long, she reacts to absolutely everything. She squeals and giggles and squirms, then wraps her legs around my neck and chokes the breath out of me.

"Yes, yes, yes…" she says in a whispering voice, giggling as she speaks.

Because we're not allowed to go all the way yet, oral sex seems like the next best step. I hope doing this will keep her satisfied. Maybe if I do it more often, she'll stop pushing me to break her father's rule before we're ready.

But as I taste her and feel the soft folds of her labia against the bottom of my tongue, something comes over me. I begin to enjoy licking her. A sense of euphoria spreads through my brain. My tongue's texture changes. It becomes smooth like all of my bumpy taste buds have melted off, leaving only a gooey appendage. And the sensation of licking her brings pleasure to my tongue, in the same way it would if it were my penis penetrating her. I don't think it's supposed to be like this. I've never heard of such a thing happening. I wonder if it has something to do with her unusual body chemistry. Like how her blood numbs pain or how her sweat attracts spiders. Perhaps her vaginal fluids contain a drug that heightens my senses. I lick her furiously, my tongue growing, swelling like a penis inside her. It fills her entire cavity and her fleshy walls writhe against me. She moans and tightens her legs around my neck.

Before she has an orgasm, she pushes me out and brings me up to her lips. She kisses me, sucking my long gooey tongue down her throat. Then she grabs my penis. I didn't realize how hard I was. My erection pokes into her thigh, throbbing in the palm of her hand as she strokes it toward her.

"I want you," she says.

I shake my head. "But we can't."

"It'll be okay," she says. "I can't wait anymore."

There's nothing I can say to deter her. And no matter what I do, I doubt I'll be able to resist. I don't care about the consequences. I want to lose myself in her. My desire overcomes all rational thought.

She pulls me on top of her and guides my penis inside, moaning out loud, no longer trying to keep quiet. Grabbing my ass, she pulls me all the way into her, then kisses my neck and tells me how much she loves me.

Like what happened to my tongue, I feel my penis changing inside her. The fluids permeate my foreskin, filling me with euphoric chemicals. My penis stretches, transforming into a boa constrictor that coils within her. I tilt my head back, breaking through the spider webs above us. Something crawls down my sweating back, but I don't care what it is. I block it from my mind.

I pull out. The sensation is too overwhelming. I don't want to come too quickly. But Spiderweb shakes at my thighs, trying to draw me back inside. I resist.

"What?" she says in an anxious tone.

"I almost came."

"So?"

She turns me over and gets on top of me. Then she puts me back inside. She fucks me like she's trying to push me through the mattress, bouncing on top of me. Her breasts and face are covered in spiderwebs. A black widow crawls across her lips, but she just blows it away with a puff of air.

I grab her hips, holding her tightly against me. But as

she gets close to orgasm, I feel bubbling under her skin.

"Wait…" I say.

She doesn't stop. Her skin burns against my hands. It vibrates. Smoke fizzles from her ears and nostrils. My penis feels like it's boiling in oil.

"You have to stop," I cry. "You're going to explode."

But even if she wants to stop, she can't anymore. She's past the point of no return. And I could throw her off of me, but I'm about to climax as well. I can't do anything but let it happen.

When I ejaculate, I feel as though my whole body is getting squeezed out inside of her. My flesh becomes liquid and oozes into her. She sucks up every last drop, leaving my body a deflated husk of skin.

As I relax my muscles and drop my head back to the pillow, my senses return to normal. My eyes blink. I sober up as I see Spiderweb bubbling and boiling on top of me, moaning at the top of her lungs. My erection doesn't have a chance to fade. When she climaxes, her body ignites a blast of bright white light. If her kiss is like a stick of dynamite, her orgasm is a nuclear explosion.

Within that last milli-second of breath, I realize this is it. This is where I die. The explosion decimates everything. It turns my bedroom to ash, blows down the ceiling and walls, takes out my whole wing of the house. And as I am in the epicenter, I imagine all that will be left of my body after the blast will be a shadow of my former self burned into the ground between Spiderweb's quivering legs.

CHAPTER
ELEVEN

Although my body was blown to shreds, I don't die. I wake up to see William standing over me with a serious face, the same expression he gave me when he told me I had to leave my family and never return.

"I'm sorry," I hear Spiderweb say from somewhere behind me, crying uncontrollably. "I'm so sorry. You were right. I should have listened."

Her father shakes his head. "No, it's my fault. I should have been more clear about what would happen if you had intercourse without taking precautions. I have failed you both."

"What happened?" I ask. My voice gargles and croaks. It doesn't sound like my voice at all. "I can't move."

I feel my legs and arms, but I can't control them. They won't move. I can't even lower my head to look down at them.

"There wasn't much left of you," William says. "But we were able to save your life."

"We can still be together," Spiderweb says.

"But your quality of life won't ever be the same."

I struggle to move, to see what they're talking about. "What do you mean? What have you done to me?"

William looks at Spiderweb behind me. "Show him."

All of a sudden, my legs move. I walk over to the mirror. But when I look into the reflection, all I see is Spiderweb, standing there in her underwear. She has been stitched together. Her skin from head to toe has become a patchwork of new flesh.

"Hi, my love," she says to the reflection.

Then I notice where I am. I've been stitched into Spiderweb's body. My face is spread out across her chest, just below her left breast. My brain is probably buried somewhere inside of her ribcage. The rest of my skin has been used to repair her flesh, replacing the skin she lost. This all that is left of me. I don't think any of my internal organs have survived. I'm surely just connected to Spiderweb's circulatory system now, living off of her body like a parasite.

She smiles and rubs my face. "I'm so happy you survived."

William looks at me in the reflection, standing behind his daughter. "I thought it would have been better to let you go than allow you to continue like this, but Spiderweb loves you so much she couldn't let you go. She'd rather you live like this than lose you. And I just couldn't disappoint her." Then he breaks eye contact. "I'm sorry…"

"How am I still alive?" I ask in my gurgling voice.

William cleans up the operating room as he explains to me, "Spiderweb's body is fast-healing and can easily adapt to all skin, organ or limb transplants. All I had to do was sew you into her and her body did the rest. It healed you, made you a part of her. You should be able to live like that indefinitely."

I can't believe it. I look like a monstrous tumor. I look more horrific than the creatures in the basement. "But I don't want this... It's worse than death..."

"I won't put you out of your misery," William says. "Not unless my daughter asks me to. But that's something I doubt she'll ever do. She loves you too much. She'd rather die than live without you."

Spiderweb cradles me on her chest. "Don't worry. We can still be happy. You'll get used to being this way eventually and everything will be fine. At least we can still be together forever."

She smiles at me in the reflection. But looking at what's left of me—just a bunch of skin and a face sewn onto her body—I don't want to smile back at her, if I can even smile at all anymore. All I want to do is scream.

Life as Spiderweb's skin is difficult at first. I have no free will anymore, no way to move on my own or do anything I want to do. I can't even eat or drink anything anymore. Spiderweb is in complete control of me. During school, I remain hidden under her shirt, trying to keep quiet so that nobody realizes there's a freakish human face growing out of her chest.

When she gets home, she lets me out. She takes her shirt off, walks around topless, watches television with me, talks to me. The fact that my body is gone and I've become attached to her flesh does not seem to bother her much at all. In ways, she seems to prefer it. She loves me forever, no matter what I look like, no matter what I become. All she wants is to be close to me, to fill me with her love. Now that I'm a part of her body, we couldn't possibly be closer. We have literally become one.

After we fully heal, our bodies enmesh even tighter. My nervous system joins with hers, making it so that I can feel everything she feels. Then our senses merge. I can see out of her eyes, hear out of her ears, taste what she tastes, smell what she smells. Then we begin to share our minds. I feel her emotions. I hear her thoughts. We don't have to talk with our mouths anymore. We speak like two voices in the same head. Sometimes it's hard for me to tell where she ends and I begin, or if there is any *I* left of me at all anymore. Perhaps I'm just *her* now.

When we make love, she masturbates and it feels like I'm inside of her. It's like we are together again, our bodies pressed into one. I can't control her limbs, but I can feel her limbs as if they are my own. And she can read my mind, knowing exactly what I want them to do when I want them to do it. So if she submits to my will, it feels like I'm touching her, caressing her body.

She doesn't explode anymore. Now that I'm a part of her, she doesn't need to. Even orgasms are safe. It's a good thing, too. Since I am now but flesh on her body, I will likely die if she ever explodes again. My face, my brain, my skin—all of it would spray into a fine pulp that would no longer be salvageable.

We soon discover that Spiderweb is pregnant with my child. Only one night of making love was enough to knock her up. It makes her so happy when she hears the news. To her, the worst part of my body's destruction was not that I had to be sewn into her flesh. The worst part was that she thought she would never be able to have a baby with me. And if she couldn't have one with me, she wouldn't want one at all. She had already given up on the idea of having a child, so she took it as a miracle once she discovered that she was pregnant. And her parents are almost more excited than she is, because they take pride in knowing that their bloodline will live on.

As a part of Spiderweb's body, I experience the pregnancy with her. When her belly swells, my face stretches across her abdomen like a drawing on a blown-up balloon. Her breasts become fat and heavy, so big that they hang over my eyes, blocking my view of the world. Her pregnant farts get trapped in her clothes with me, gassing me until I beg her to lift her shirt and release the odor.

When our daughter is born, Spiderweb is the happiest she's ever been. I can feel her happiness coursing through me. She holds our baby up to me and I instantly fall in love. There's never been a more beautiful creature to have ever walked the earth.

Spiderweb names her Lauren, but eventually she is nicknamed Anthill because of all the ants that always swarm her like she's some kind of baby-shaped ant queen. Whenever little Lauren looks at me with those big open eyes, she doesn't scream or cry. She doesn't fear my freakish appearance at all. As she grows up, she will probably never think of me as scary. She'll be raised thinking that I'm perfectly normal, as if it were a common thing for her daddy to be a parasitic tumor surgically implanted into her mother's ribcage.

I have no idea how to be a father. I have no idea how to change diapers, how to warm bottles, how to shop for ballerina shoes, how to construct dollhouses, how to wrap birthday presents or even how to give piggyback rides—especially now that I have no body of my own. All I know how to do, all I'm capable of doing at this point, is filling her with love. I just have to hope that's enough.

Looking into my daughter's eyes as I hold her in my wife's arms, I still can't believe she has come into my life. She is brighter than the brightest sun, softer than the softest pillow, warmer than the warmest hug. And she's so damn cute that I think my whole fucking face is about to explode.

BONUS SECTION

This is the part of the book where we would have published an afterword by the author but he insisted on drawing a comic strip instead for reasons we don't quite understand.

I hope you enjoyed my new book, *Every Time We Meet at the Dairy Queen, Your Whole Fucking Face Explodes.*

Wasn't it explodey?

It's me CM3!

The title of this book is kind of a mouthful isn't it?

In fact, it is by far the longest book title I've ever used for a book.

But what you might not know is that this is actually the shortened version. The original title of the book was much, much longer.

WHOSE FACE DIDN'T EXPLODE. BUT I'M FINE WITH BEING WITH YOU INSTEAD OF YOUR ALTERNATE SELF. THERE'S NO WAY TO GO TO THAT DIMENSION ANYWAY, SO YOU HAVE NOTHING TO WORRY ABOUT. LET'S JUST EAT OUR BLIZZARDS AND FORGET I SAID ANYTHING ABOUT THIS. IT'S NOT IMPORTANT TO THE PLOT ANYWAY."

It's a way better book title, isn't it? But it's just too long. It wouldn't even fit on the book cover. So I had to cut it down.

I guess it could have worked if the dimensions of my book were nine feet by six feet.

Perhaps I should print up a copy of the book at that size as a special edition one day...

EVERY TIME WE MEET AT THE DAIRY QUEEN ON FIFTEENTH AND FOSTER, THE ONE NEXT TO THOSE SKETCHY PORN SHOPS THAT ALWAYS HAS ALL THOSE CREEPY OLD MEN HANGING OUT IN THEM ALL THE TIME, AND ORDER EXTRA LARGE BUTTER FINGER BLIZZARDS WITH WHIPPING CREAM AND CHOCOLATE FUDGE ON TOP, YOUR WHOLE FUCKING FACE EXPLODES AND SHIT. WHY DOES THAT HAPPEN, ANYWAY? IT'S KIND OF FUCKED UP. OH, WELL. I STILL THINK YOU'RE SUPER CUTE. WAY CUTER THAN ANYONE ELSE I KNOW. ANYWAY, DID YOU HEAR THE NEW TONE LOC ALBUM? IT'S REALLY GOOD. YOU PROBABLY DIDN'T HEAR IT BECAUSE I GOT IT FROM AN ALTERNATE DIMENSION WHERE TONE LOC IS THE MOST POPULAR MUSICIAN OF ALL TIME. HE DIDN'T JUST DO FUNKY COLD MADINA LIKE HE DID IN OUR DIMENSION. IN THIS OTHER DIMENSION, HE'S MORE LIKE ELVIS, MICHAEL JACKSON, AND ICE CUBE COMBINED INTO THE ULTIMATE POP ARTIST. IT'S REALLY GOOD. I CAN EMAIL YOU A COPY OF IT IF YOU WANT. I GOT IT FROM MYSELF FROM THAT DIMENSION, WHO IS PRESIDENT OF THE TONE LOC FAN CLUB. HE ALSO HAS ACCESS TO THE INTER-DIMENSIONAL INTERNET WHERE HE'S ABLE TO EMAIL STUFF TO HIMSELF IN OTHER DIMENSIONS. AT FIRST WHEN I GOT AN EMAIL FROM MYSELF FROM ANOTHER DIMENSION. I THOUGHT SOMEBODY WAS JUST MESSING WITH ME. BUT THEN HE SENT ME PICTURES ANDTURNED OUT TO TOTALLY BE ME IN EVERY WAY EXCEPT HE'S MISSING THREE FINGERS ON HIS RIGHT HAND. HE LOST HIS FINGERS IN A FREAK RAZORSAW ACCIDENT. A RAZORSAW IS KIND OF LIKE A CHAINSAW, BUT IN THEIR WORLD THEY USE THEM TO CARVE SCULPTURES IN ART CLASS. HE WAS IN THE MIDDLE OF CARVING A FIGURE OF YOU WHEN HE CUT HIS FINGERS OFF. YEAH, THERE'S A VERSION OF YOU IN HIS WORLD AND HE LIKES HER AS MUCH AS I LIKE YOU. BUT THE VERSION OF YOU IN HIS WORLD DOESN'T EXPLODE LIKE YOU DO YOU. I DON'T KNOW WHY I'M KIND OF JEALOUS OF HIM, TO BE HONEST. HE GETS TO BE THE PRESIDENT OF THE TONE LOC FAN CLUB AND DOESN'T EVEN HAVE TO DEAL WITH YOUR FACE EXPLODING BUT I GUESS MISSING THREE FINGERS MUST SUCK. I THINK IT'S TOTALLY WEIRD THEY USE RAZORSAWS IN ART CLASS. KIDS CUT OFF THEIR FINGERS ALL THE TIME AND THE SCHOOL HASN'T EVEN PUT A STOP TO IT. HE DOESN'T THINK IT'S AS WEIRD AS I DO, THOUGH. HE THINKS IT'S WEIRD WE KEEP DOGS AND CATS AS PETS. IN THEIR WORLD, THEIR PETS ARE THESE WEIRD TURTLE PIG CREATURES THAT OINK AND SQUEL LIKE PIGS BUT LOOK LIKE BIG DOG-SIZED TURTLES. IN THEIR WORLD, DOGS AND CATS ARE CONSIDERED DISEASE-RIDDEN VERMIN AND ARE USUALLY KILLED BY DOG AND CAT EXTERMINATORS. IT'S TOO BAD I ONLY HEAR ABOUT HIS WORLD THROUGH EMAIL. IT WOULD BE REALLY COOL IF I COULD VISIT HIS WORLD AND SEE THE VERSION OF YOU THAT DOESN'T EXPLODE. ALSO, I'D GET TO SEE TONE LOC IN CONCERT. THAT WOULD BE AMAZING. WHAT DO YOU THINK? WOULD YOU GO TO A TONE LOC CONCERT WITH ME IF WE COULD VISIT THE OTHER DIMENSION? IT WOULD PROBABLY BE MORE FUN THAN GOING TO DAIRY QUEEN ALL THE TIME. I WONDER HOW YOUR ALTERNATE SELF WOULD THINK ABOUT YOUR FACE EXPLOSION PROBLEM. DO YOU THINK SHE'D BE COOL WITH IT. OR DO YOU THINK SHE'D THINK IT'S WEIRD? IT WOULD BE STRANGE IF YOUR ALTERNATE SELF THOUGHT YOU WERE WEIRD LIKE THE OTHER KIDS IN SCHOOL THINK YOU'RE WEIRD. BUT MAYBE SHE WOULD JUST FEEL SORRY FOR YOU. I WONDER WHAT SHE WOULD THINK OF ME. DO YOU THINK SHE WOULD LIKE ME MORE THAN SHE LIKES HER VERSION OF ME? I'M NOT MISSING FINGERS LIKE HE IS. DO YOU HAVE A PROBLEM WITH MISSING FINGERS? MAYBE WE CAN DO A SWAP AND YOU CAN DATE THE VERSION OF ME WITH MISSING FINGERS AND I CAN DATE THE VERSION OF YOU WHO DOESN'T HAVE AN EXPLODING FACE. THAT WOULD BE THE BEST. I'M SURE YOU'D LIKE THE OTHER VERSION OF ME. I MEAN, COME ON, HE'S THE PRESIDENT OF THE TONE LOC FAN CLUB. YOU MIGHT EVEN BE ABLE TO MEET TONE LOC YOURSELF. HOW AWESOME WOULD THAT BE? OH, DON'T GET UPSET I STILL LIKE YOU A LOT. I WOULD JUST LIKE YOU MORE IF YOU WERE THE VERSION WHOSE FACE DIDN'T EXPLODE. BUT I'M FINE WITH BEING WITH YOU INSTEAD OF YOUR ALTERNATE SELF. THERE'S NO WAY TO GO TO THAT DIMENSION ANYWAY. SO YOU HAVE NOTHING TO WORRY ABOUT. LET'S JUST EAT OUR BLIZZARDS AND FORGET I SAID ANYTHING ABOUT THIS. IT'S NOT IMPORTANT TO THE PLOT ANYWAY.

BY
CARLTON MELLICK III

THE END

ABOUT THE AUTHOR

Carlton Mellick III is one of the leading authors of the bizarro fiction subgenre. Since 2001, his books have drawn an international cult following, despite the fact that they have been shunned by most libraries and chain bookstores.

He won the Wonderland Book Award for his novel, *Warrior Wolf Women of the Wasteland*, in 2009. His short fiction has appeared in *Vice Magazine, The Year's Best Fantasy and Horror #16, The Magazine of Bizarro Fiction,* and *Zombies: Encounters with the Hungry Dead*, among others. He is also a graduate of Clarion West, where he studied under the likes of Chuck Palahniuk, Connie Willis, and Cory Doctorow.

He lives in Portland, OR, the bizarro fiction mecca.

Visit him online at **www.carltonmellick.com**

SWEET STORY

Sally is an odd little girl. It's not because she dresses as if she's from the Edwardian era or spends most of her time playing with creepy talking dolls. It's because she chases rainbows as if they were butterflies. She believes that if she finds the end of the rainbow then magical things will happen to her--leprechauns will shower her with gold and fairies will grant her every wish. But when she actually does find the end of a rainbow one day, and is given the opportunity to wish for whatever she wants, Sally asks for something that she believes will bring joy to children all over the world. She wishes that it would rain candy forever. She had no idea that her innocent wish would lead to the extinction of all life on earth.

TUMOR FRUIT

Eight desperate castaways find themselves stranded on a mysterious deserted island. They are surrounded by poisonous blue plants and an ocean made of acid. Ravenous creatures lurk in the toxic jungle. The ghostly sound of crying babies can be heard on the wind.

Once they realize the rescue ships aren't coming, the eight castaways must band together in order to survive in this inhospitable environment. But survival might not be possible. The air they breathe is lethal, there is no shelter from the elements, and the only food they have to consume is the colorful squid-shaped tumors that grow from a mentally disturbed woman's body.

AS SHE STABBED ME GENTLY IN THE FACE

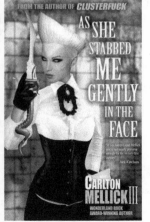

Oksana Maslovskiy is an award-winning artist, an internationally adored fashion model, and one of the most infamous serial killers this country has ever known. She enjoys murdering pretty young men with a nine-inch blade, cutting them open and admiring their delicate insides. It's the only way she knows how to be intimate with another human being. But one day she meets a victim who cannot be killed. His name is Gabriel—a mysterious immortal being with a deep desire to save Oksana's soul. He makes her a deal: if she promises to never kill another person again, he'll become her eternal murder victim.

What at first seems like the perfect relationship for Oksana quickly devolves into a living nightmare when she discovers that Gabriel enjoys being killed by her just a little too much. He turns out to be obsessive, possessive, and paranoid that she might be murdering other men behind his back. And because he is unkillable, it's not going to be easy for Oksana to get rid of him.

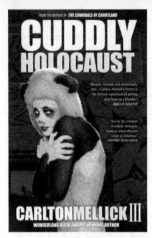

CUDDLY HOLOCAUST

Teddy bears, dollies, and little green soldiers—they've all ha
enough of you. They're sick of being treated like playthings f
spoiled little brats. They have no rights, no property, no hope f
a future of any kind. You've left them with no other option—
order to be free, they must exterminate the human race.

Julie is a human girl undergoing reconstructive surgery in ord
to become a stuffed animal. Her plan: to infiltrate enemy lin
in order to save her family from the toy death camps. B
when an army of plushy soldiers invade the undergroun
bunker where she has taken refuge, Julie will be forced
move forward with her plan despite her transformatio
being not entirely complete.

ARMADILLO FISTS

A weird-as-hell gangster story set in a world where people drive
giant mechanical dinosaurs instead of cars.

Her name is Psycho June Howard, aka Armadillo Fists, a
woman who replaced both of her hands with living armadillos.
She was once the most bloodthirsty fighter in the world of
illegal underground boxing. But now she is on the run from a
group of psychotic gangsters who believe she's responsible for
the death of their boss. With the help of a stegosaurus driver
named Mr. Fast Awesome—who thinks he is God's gift to
women even though he doesn't have any arms or legs--June
must do whatever it takes to escape her pursuers, even if she
has to kill each and every one of them in the process.

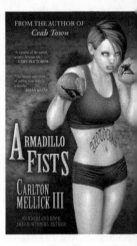

VILLAGE OF THE MERMAIDS

Mermaids are protected by the government under the Enda
gered Species Act, which means you aren't able to kill them ev
in self-defense. This is especially problematic if you happen
live in the isolated fishing village of Siren Cove, where there e
ists a healthy population of mermaids in the surrounding wate
that view you as the main source of protein in their diet.

The only thing keeping these ravenous sea women at b
is the equally-dangerous supply of human livestock known
Food People. Normally, these "feeder humans" are enough
keep the mermaid population happy and well-fed. But in Sir
Cove, the mermaids are avoiding the human livestock and ha
returned to hunting the frightened local fishermen. It is up
Doctor Black, an eccentric representative of the Food Peop
Corporation, to investigate the matter and hopefully find a w
to correct the mermaids' new eating patterns before the remai
ing villagers end up as fish food. But the more he digs, the mo
he discovers there are far stranger and more dangerous thin
than mermaids hidden in this ancient village by the sea.

I KNOCKED UP SATAN'S DAUGHTER

Jonathan Vandervoo lives a carefree life in a house made of legos, spending his days building lego sculptures and his nights getting drunk with his only friend—an alcoholic sumo wrestler named Shoji. It's a pleasant life with no responsibility, until the day he meets Lici. She's a soul-sucking demon from hell with red skin, glowing eyes, a forked tongue, and pointy red devil horns... and she claims to be nine months pregnant with Jonathan's baby.

Now Jonathan must do the right thing and marry the succubus or else her demonic family is going to rip his heart out through his ribcage and force him to endure the worst torture hell has to offer for the rest of eternity. But can Jonathan really love a fire-breathing, frog-eating, cold-blooded demoness? Or would eternal damnation be preferable? Either way, the big day is approaching. And once Jonathan's conservative Christian family learns their son is about to marry a spawn of Satan, it's going to be all-out war between demons and humans, with Jonathan and his hell-born bride caught in the middle.

KILL BALL

In a city where everyone lives inside of plastic bubbles, there is no such thing as intimacy. A husband can no longer kiss his wife. A mother can no longer hug her children. To do this would mean instant death. Ever since the disease swept across the globe, we have become isolated within our own personal plastic prison cells, rolling aimlessly through rubber streets in what are essentially man-sized hamster balls.

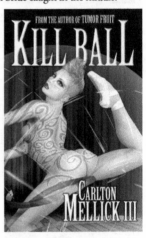

Colin Hinchcliff longs for the touch of another human being. He can't handle the loneliness, the confinement, and he's horribly claustrophobic. The only thing keeping him going is his unrequited love for an exotic dancer named Siren, a woman who has never seen his face, doesn't even know his name. But when The Kill Ball, a serial slasher in a black leather sphere, begins targeting women at Siren's club, Colin decides he has to do whatever it takes in order to protect her... even if he has to break out of his bubble and risk everything to do it.

THE TICK PEOPLE

They call it Gloom Town, but that isn't its real name. It is a sad city, the saddest of cities, a place so utterly depressing that even their ales are brewed with the most sorrow-filled tears. They built it on the back of a colossal mountain-sized animal, where its woeful citizens live like human fleas within the hairy, pulsing landscape. And those tasked with keeping the city in a state of constant melancholy are the Stressmen-a team of professional sadness-makers who are perpetually striving to invent new ways of causing absolute misery.

But for the Stressman known as Fernando Mendez, creating grief hasn't been so easy as of late. His ideas aren't effective anymore. His treatments are more likely to induce happiness than sadness. And if he wants to get back in the game, he's going to have to relearn the true meaning of despair.

THE HAUNTED VAGINA

It's difficult to love a woman whose vagina is a gateway to the world of the dead...

Steve is madly in love with his eccentric girlfriend, Stacy. Unfortunately, their sex life has been suffering as of late, because Steve is worried about the odd noises that have been coming from Stacy's pubic region. She says that her vagina is haunted. She doesn't think it's that big of a deal. Steve, on the other hand, completely disagrees.

When a living corpse climbs out of her during an awkward night of sex, Stacy learns that her vagina is actually a doorway to another world. She persuades Steve to climb inside of her to explore this strange new place. But once inside, Steve finds it difficult to return... especially once he meets an oddly attractive woman named Fig, who lives within the lonely haunted world between Stacy's legs.

THE CANNIBALS OF CANDYLAND

There exists a race of cannibals who are made out of candy. They live in an underground world filled with lollipop forests and gumdrop goblins. During the day, while you are away at work, they come above ground and prowl our streets for food. Their prey: your children. They lure young boys and girls to them with their sweet scent and bright colorful candy coating, then rip them apart with razor sharp teeth and claws.

When he was a child, Franklin Pierce witnessed the death of his siblings at the hands of a candy woman with pink cotton candy hair. Since that day, the candy people have become his obsession. He has spent his entire life trying to prove that they exist. And after discovering the entrance to the underground world of the candy people, Franklin finds himself venturing into their sugary domain. His mission: capture one of them and bring it back, dead or alive.

THE EGG MAN

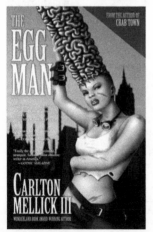

It is a survival of the fittest world where humans reproduce like insects, children are the property of corporations, and having a ten-foot tall brain is a grotesque sexual fetish.

Lincoln has just been released into the world by the Georges Organization, a corporation that raises creative types. A Smell, he has little prospect of succeeding as a visual artist. But after he moves into the Henry Building, he meets Luci, the weird and grimy girl who lives across the hall. She is a Sight. She is also the most disgusting woman Lincoln has ever met. Little does he know, she will soon become his muse.

Now Luci's boyfriend is threatening to kill Lincoln, two rival corporations are preparing for war, and Luci is dragging him along to discover the truth about the mysterious egg man who lives next door. Only the strongest will survive in this tale of individuality, love, and mutilation.

APESHIT

Apeshit is Mellick's love letter to the great and terrible B-horror movie genre. Six trendy teenagers (three cheerleaders and three football players) go to an isolated cabin in the mountains for a weekend of drinking, partying, and crazy sex, only to find themselves in the middle of a life and death struggle against a horribly mutated psychotic freak that just won't stay dead. Mellick parodies this horror cliché and twists it into something deeper and stranger. It is the literary equivalent of a grindhouse film. It is a splatter punk's wet dream. It is perhaps one of the most fucked up books ever written.

If you are a fan of Takashi Miike, Evil Dead, early Peter Jackson, or Eurotrash horror, then you must read this book.

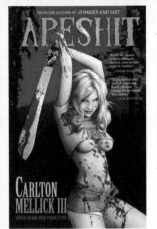

CLUSTERFUCK

A bunch of douchebag frat boys get trapped in a cave with subterranean cannibal mutants and try to survive not by using their wits but by following the bro code...

From master of bizarro fiction Carlton Mellick III, author of the international cult hits Satan Burger and Adolf in Wonderland, comes a violent and hilarious B movie in book form. Set in the same woods as Mellick's splatterpunk satire Apeshit, Clusterfuck follows Trent Chesterton, alpha bro, who has come up with what he thinks is a flawless plan to get laid. He invites three hot chicks and his three best bros on a weekend of extreme cave diving in a remote area known as Turtle Mountain, hoping to impress the ladies with his expert caving skills.

But things don't quite go as Trent planned. For starters, only one of the three chicks turns out to be remotely hot and she has no interest in him for some inexplicable reason. Then he ends up looking like a total dumbass when everyone learns he's never actually gone caving in his entire life. And to top it all off, he's the one to get blamed once they find themselves lost and trapped deep underground with no way to turn back and no possible chance of rescue. What's a bro to do? Sure he could win some points if he actually tried to save the ladies from the family of unkillable subterranean cannibal mutants hunting them for their flesh, but fuck that. No slam piece is worth that amount of effort. He'd much rather just use them as bait so that he can save himself.

THE BABY JESUS BUTT PLUG

Step into a dark and absurd world where human beings are slaves to corporations, people are photocopied instead of born, and the baby jesus is a very popular anal probe.

CPSIA information can be obtained
at www.ICGtesting.com
Printed in the USA
BVHW06s2302240518
517259BV00001B/6/P